I0733474

Trust in Truth

EMILY BANTING

Trust in Truth
Copyright © 2021 Emily Banting
Published by Sapphfic Publishing
ISBN: 978-1-915157-03-4
First edition: December 2021

This is a work of fiction. Names, characters, business, events and incidents are the products of the author's imagination. Any resemblance to actual persons, living or dead, or actual events is purely coincidental.

All Rights Reserved. This book, or parts thereof, may not be reproduced in any form without permission of the author.

CREDITS:
Editor: Hatch Editorial

1 3 4 5 6 7 8 9 10

ABOUT THE AUTHOR

As a sapphic author and screenwriter, I'm passionate about increasing the representation of sapphic women over forty in literature and on-screen.

I write about women in their prime, experiencing everything life throws at them - missed opportunities: regret: lost loves: family problems: aching joints: and menopause.

I have a passion and a degree in Archaeology and Heritage Management, so I never miss an opportunity to sneak historic buildings into my books. The Nunswick Abbey Series features a Georgian country house, a quaint historic village setting and of course, oodles of ruined abbey.

When I'm not hiding behind my MacBook pretending to write whilst secretly consuming tea and biscuits, I bow to the unreasonable demands of my cat overlord and walk my starving, velcro Labrador.

FIND ME HERE

I love to hear from my readers. If you would like to get in touch you can find me here…

www.emilybanting.co.uk

Or follow me here…

facebook.com / emilybantingauthor
instagram.com / emilybanting
twitter.com / emily_banting
bookbub.com / authors / emily-banting
goodreads.com / emily_banting
amazon.com / author / emilybanting

ACKNOWLEDGMENTS

Thank you to everyone who got in touch or left a review after reading my debut novel *Lost in Love.* Your enthusiasm, appreciation and demands for more of Anna and Katherine spur me on whilst I'm writing book three. I hope you will be patient with me as I carve out their future and that you won't be too mad at me IF this is their last book. I have so many other characters that want their stories told in 2022.

Thanks go as always to my amazing team of BETA and ARC readers, and my wonderful editor Jess – I couldn't do this without you all. Special thanks go to Laure Dherbécourt for proofreading — and so much more.

Lastly, thank you to my readers and the wider lesfic community for opening your arms and welcoming me in. I have felt quite overwhelmed with the encouragement and support from readers and fellow authors since the release of my debut.

CHAPTER 1

$\mathcal{A}$nna stretched back in her chair and yawned; it was the end of a very long week. Today marked the first closure day of the winter season at Nunswick Abbey. The site was so tranquil without visitors; a walk around the ruined walls of the abbey could transport you anywhere in time. Not that she'd had time for walking today; she'd been stuck in her office since her arrival that morning.

The closure of the site signified a turning point for Anna — the promise of a new job. The position of marketing and events manager would be created in the new year, and she was determined to make it hers. Although she was technically still tour supervisor until the site reopened in the spring, Anna had been asked by the trustees to put on a New Year's Eve event at the abbey as a trial run. If she made a success of it, she hoped it would impress the trustees enough to give her the job.

As much as she loved her tour supervisor role, her background had been in marketing and events, and she missed the buzz of it. Her biggest regret was moving away from it. She'd relocated to move in with Jessica, her ex-girlfriend, which meant a change of job. Jessica had said she could support her whilst she found a new job that suited her. A week later she had been made redundant forcing Anna to find any job she could.

Her position as a researcher at the National Archives had fortunately proved invaluable. Not only had she learned a new set of skills, she believed it was what enticed the trustees to hire her when she moved back to Nunswick. They then went on to trust her to create the tour and write a guidebook, which was now on its second print run. She knew the abbey like the back of her hand, in her mind there was no one better to market it.

Although she had been planning the New Year's Eve event alongside her other duties, there was still a lot to organise in the four weeks she had left. Now she finally felt able to focus one hundred percent on it. The pressure was already on without the interruption Christmas would bring.

A ping from her laptop alerted her to an email; she hoped it was the one she was waiting for from the branding agency. It was. She opened the attachment, excited to see their ideas for the branding of Abbey Barn. They were excellent considering the restrictions of the Nunswick Abbey branding they were asked to work around. It needed to be complementary to the abbey and have its own unique style at the same time.

They had sent a couple of options; one caught her eye that incorporated a sketch of the medieval barn. Its aesthetics were the unique selling point. She was keen to get home and show the designs to Katherine. Until she was officially appointed into the new role, all decisions had to go past Katherine who was the trustee overseeing the barn renovation and its management.

She shut the lid of her laptop, extracted her bag from under her desk, and turned out the light. It was her turn to lock up, and she had a vigorous checking system in place to avoid any repeats of her costly mistake from the summer. She checked the larger office next to hers to make sure the lights were off. Margaret had appointed this as the trustees' office with hot desks, despite only Margaret and Katherine having paid roles onsite. As she closed the door, the movement of air wafted the scent of Katherine's perfume that dominated the room despite her absence. She inhaled deeply and smiled; she adored the aroma.

The smaller office was temporarily shared by Carrie and Anna. They were due to move into the two ground-floor offices in the barn once it was finally fitted out next year. Anna couldn't wait; it would mean Katherine would move into their old office away from Margaret.

Although Margaret was Anna's boss, she had felt uneasy towards her since she'd propositioned Katherine. Katherine had just begun her role as an abbey trustee, and Anna and Katherine had just got back together after the General Medical Council debacle, when Margaret had left some flowers on Katherine's doorstep with a dinner invitation. Katherine had immediately set Margaret straight, and Margaret had said there was no impropriety intended; she was simply reaching out in friendship as they would be working together.

Anna still didn't trust her. She had witnessed

Margaret's behaviour over the last few months since Katherine had taken on the role of trustee, and it was obvious to her that Margaret sought more than friendship with Katherine. It had recently crossed her mind that Margaret had informed the General Medical Council of her and Katherine's relationship to split them up. She had no evidence, of course, and was unlikely to ever have any. Realising her heart rate was picking up, Anna pushed the thoughts to the back of her mind. She locked the gate to the abbey car park and began the short walk home to Abbey House.

As she lifted her key to the door, it was opened for her by Katherine, strapped into her cooking apron as was usual of an evening. She placed a kiss on Anna's cheek as she entered. Anna would never tire of coming home to her.

"It's here," Katherine said with a hint of melody in her voice.

Anna looked up at the enormous Christmas tree. It filled the space in front of the staircase and extended upwards to the first-floor landing. Her mouth dropped open. "Did they not have any big ones?"

Katherine nudged her. "It's fine. It fits perfectly."

"How do we even decorate it?"

"You on the stairs and me on the stepladder of course," Katherine replied flatly.

"You mean you on the stairs and me on the stepladder."

Katherine nudged her again. "Don't be cheeky, young lady. I think I can manage a stepladder."

"I'm sure you can, however, I can manage it better. I have flat shoes on for a start."

"Fair enough," Katherine said, scrunching her face.

A rustling from within the tree made Anna jump back in fright. Virginia jumped out and landed at her feet.

"Virginia!" Katherine shook her head at her and shooed her away. "The silly cat keeps hiding in there." She rummaged in a large box of decorations that lay beside the tree. "Tinsel first?"

"Whatever you say, boss. It's been a long time since I decorated a tree."

A line etched between Katherine's eyebrows. "I'm going to need more information."

Anna shrugged. "I'm just not a very Christmassy person. I don't normally bother with any of this." She bit her lip. "Please don't tell me you went to all this trouble for me."

Katherine grinned and threw some tinsel at Anna, which she caught. "Of course not. I love Christmas and I always go to this much trouble, regardless of ungrateful house guests."

Anna sucked in a breath through her teeth. "Harsh. I'll have you know I am very grateful for all the services I receive in this house." She threw the tinsel around Katherine's neck and pulled her gently towards her, planting a kiss on her lips.

Katherine reciprocated and pulled Anna's body tightly against hers. "Maybe you just need the spirit of Christmas put in you."

Anna's right eyebrow shot up. "Oh, did you buy us a new toy?"

Katherine stifled a giggle. "Come on, this naked tree won't dress itself. I'll take the tinsel to the top, and you can wind it around as I lower it."

Anna did as instructed and climbed the stepladder. Katherine barked orders from above as to the best position for the tinsel, purely based on her ability to see better from high up, not because she was a perfectionist as Anna suggested.

Katherine re-joined Anna and made some minor adjustments to the tinsel. "Baubles next. Do you want to hang them?"

Anna took a step back and held her hands up in front of her. "No way am I taking on that responsibility. Plus, I don't have a tape measure to meet your exacting standards when it comes to bauble distribution."

Katherine mouth opened and she nudged her upper arm into Anna's. "Watch it, you!"

Anna set about adding the hooks to the baubles and passed them one by one to Katherine for precision hanging.

"The branding for Abbey Barn has come back. We need to give feedback ASAP so we can get the leaflet finalised and order signage. The printers will be getting busy towards Christmas."

"Can't it wait until after? It doesn't officially open until the spring. I would have thought you'd have enough on your plate with the New Year's Eve event."

"We have two hundred people coming to the abbey for the event. The barn may not look pretty on the inside, so the least we can do is make sure it looks inviting on the outside. I want them all taking a leaflet home too. If we can't rely on our supporters to book the barn for events, we are stuck out of the starting block. If you're worried the signs will get damaged when the barn is fitted out, we can take them down in the new year. We'll need a string of lights for the outside. I just need everything to be perfect if I'm going to impress the trustees and get this job."

"If it were up to me, I would have given it to you. It was Margaret who insisted on the trial run." Katherine looked at Anna's open mouth. "Perhaps I shouldn't have mentioned that."

Katherine had just confirmed what Anna had suspected. Margaret had been insistent that Anna was irreplaceable as a tour supervisor and seemed reluctant to let her organise their first big event. Anna had suspected it was because the new role would mean working closely with Katherine. The tour supervisor position was only contracted ten months out of the year, from February through November. She was sure Margaret had planned to have Katherine all to herself over those two months. Luckily Katherine had persuaded the other trustees that Anna was worth giving a chance to.

Katherine waved her hand at Anna, snapping her from her thoughts that had drifted to Katherine and Margaret alone together for two months. She shuddered.

"Bauble." Katherine held out her hand.

"Last one."

Katherine placed it on the tree and stood back to admire their work. "One last touch." She pulled an angel from the box and offered it to Anna. "Do you want to do the honours?"

Anna nodded up at the aggressive-looking crown of

the tree. "No, thank you. I'm not subjecting her to a month impaled on that spike."

Katherine twisted her lips. "Fair point." She rummaged further in the box and extracted a star. "Better?"

"Much."

"Good. Now do the honours and then I have an early present for you."

"Really?" Anna replied with a hint of trepidation.

"Yes, really. Don't tell me you don't like presents either."

"Okay, I won't." Anna ran up the stairs and placed the star on the top to a round of applause from Katherine.

Anna called down. "You take this Christmas malarkey too seriously."

"Maybe you don't take it seriously enough. Now come here and open this." Katherine extracted a present from behind the tree and passed it to Anna.

A squeeze of the elegantly wrapped present caused a lurch in Anna's stomach. "Please don't tell me this is a Christmas jumper."

"Let me guess, you don't do Christmas jumpers either?"

Anna's heart sank. She had always refused to embrace the craziness that was the Christmas jumper season. She believed it was another fad to extract money from people during an already financially difficult time. She hoped it wasn't one with flashing lights.

It took a moment to unwrap the present. First, she had to make it past the elaborately tied bow Katherine had placed around it with red ribbon. As she tore at the wrapping paper, she was relieved to extract a navy-blue jumper with a white deer on the front. She should have known that it would be tasteful and elegant if Katherine had bought it.

"I have one too, though slightly different. I'm not sure we are at the matching jumper stage of our relationship."

"Let's never reach that stage," Anna joked, placing a kiss on Katherine's cheek. "Thank you, it's lovely."

"You're welcome. Right, I'll pour us some wine, there is some left over from the beef bourguignon that's in the oven."

"You really know how to turn a girl on. I'll get changed and then show you those designs."

Katherine wagged a finger at her. "No, you won't, Miss Walker. No shop talk, please. You'll have to see me in my office on Monday morning." Katherine winked as she left the room.

That would have been quite the proposition if it wasn't for the fact that Margaret would likely be there too.

CHAPTER 2

"Have you told her yet?" Harry asked, giving Katherine a cheeky grin.

Anna looked from Harry to Katherine. "Told me what? What are you two up to?"

Katherine hadn't expected Harry to just come out with it, even though she often found older people quite blunt. She supposed it was a mixture of being a product of their time and having a lack of time left.

"I've been planning a birthday surprise for you."

Anna narrowed her eyes at Katherine. "I hate surprises."

"That's because you're a control freak. You need to work on that."

Anna's eyebrows shot up. "I'm the control freak?"

"Yes, I'm a perfectionist; they are two completely different traits," Katherine replied, impressed by her own ability to keep a straight face.

Anna scrunched her face at Katherine. "So come on, what is it?"

"I'm taking you away to Bath for the weekend." Katherine held her breath, unsure what response it would elicit from Anna. Harry had assured her that his daughter would be pleased.

Anna nodded.

Katherine found it difficult to read her. She was relieved to see her straight lips form into a smile.

"I can't help but think someone had a hand in that decision, Dad."

"Well, she asked, I just couldn't remember if you ever went with that, oh, what's her name."

"Jessica, Dad," Anna replied, rolling her eyes.

"Yeah, her."

"No, I have never been to Bath. It will be my pleasure to join you on a weekend away. I thank you."

Katherine grinned at her tone.

"See, told you, doc."

"Dad, you can't call her that. She's not a doctor anymore."

"Technically I'm still qualified," Katherine quickly added under her breath.

Anna gave her a look that told her she wasn't helping.

"She'll always be the doc to me. You don't mind do you, doc?"

Katherine leaned forward and tapped his hand lightly. "I've never minded, Harry." She noticed how his speech had become more monotone since she'd first seen him as a patient. It had always been slow and soft, now he appeared to be losing vocal range. She made a mental note to check what vocal therapy he was receiving, if any.

"So is this next weekend?" Anna asked.

"Yes, before everything starts getting crazy with Christmas, New Year, and reopening. No laptops allowed!"

Anna's lips parted and Katherine anticipated her reply. "No ifs or buts."

Anna scowled at Katherine in response.

"Are you sure you'll be okay if we miss visiting you, Dad?"

"Of course. You young'uns go and have fun."

"We'll call you instead," Anna added.

"All right, love, only if you have time."

"So you're coming to us for Christmas, Harry?" Katherine said. "They've agreed you can stay one night."

Harry's face lit up. "Yes, please, doc. I'm really looking forward to it."

Katherine felt a little teary at his comment.

"It's been too long since I had a cuddle with Virginia," he added. He chuckled at Katherine as her face fell in disappointment. "Only joking."

Katherine rolled her eyes at him. "Virginia might not win the battle with the Christmas tree, so there are no guarantees she'll make it to Christmas Day. My friend will be there, Rebecca, you've met her before."

"Yes, I remember. Big, scary barrister lady."

Katherine couldn't help but laugh at his summation of Rebecca. She'd have to relay that to her when they spoke next.

"Tell me, Harry, why is your daughter so disinterested in Christmas?" Katherine felt frustrated that Anna didn't share her enthusiasm. It was her first Christmas in a very long time where she would be able to really enjoy it. Previous holidays had involved either working or being on call. She couldn't even remember the last Christmas when she'd had a drink. In more recent years she'd not even had anyone to share it with.

"We've never been big Christmas people. We're not religious, doc."

"Well, neither am I, but I can still find joy in the festivities."

Harry leaned forward. "I'll let you into a secret."

Katherine inched closer to him.

"Dad, I don't think Kat needs to hear this story."

Katherine's eyes widened and she let out a chuckle. "I think I do."

"When Anna was six, she caught me putting the Christmas presents under the tree."

"Yes, that's enough, thank you, Dad," Anna said, loudly attempting to drown him out.

"Go on, Harry," Katherine said, encouraging him despite the blush forming on Anna's face.

"I tried to convince her that I was just checking Father Christmas had been and was tidying up the presents, but she interrogated me."

Katherine lifted an eyebrow at Anna. "I bet she did."

Anna folded her arms and rolled her eyes.

"She wouldn't be convinced any other way and said if there wasn't a Father Christmas, then she would have his mince pie and special juice. Before I realised, she'd reached for the whisky and downed it. Her face was a picture, and the day after she was a little worse for wear. Admittedly, it was a very large one."

"That's why you won't drink whisky!" Katherine said, trying to contain her laughter.

"Thank you, Dad." Anna got up from her chair and stretched. "Time we left you in peace, I think." She leaned over and placed a kiss on Harry's head.

Katherine took her cue, despite wanting to stay and listen to Harry's tales.

"Go on then, be off with you. I've got plenty more stories to tell, doc, if you want to hear them sometime." He reached up to Katherine and took her hand.

"I do, Harry."

He squeezed her hand and pulled her towards him. "Good luck with it, doc," he whispered.

Katherine squeezed back. "Thanks, Harry."

The smell of Sunday lunch hit them as they made their way out.

Anna inhaled noisily. "I want to live here."

Katherine laughed and linked her arm through Anna's. "You are quite the convert to a care home, aren't you? Come on, let's go to the pub, and I'll buy you lunch. I'll drive!" She knew there would be no challenge as Anna did most of the driving now.

"Why was Dad wishing you luck?" Anna asked as she clicked in her seat belt.

Katherine smirked. "I don't know, perhaps he was referring to me having to spend a whole weekend in Bath with you."

Anna scowled. "Is Margaret all right with us having time off... *together*?"

"Of course. Why do you have to say it like that?"

"Like what?" Anna replied causally.

"Together," Katherine replied in an identical tone to Anna.

Anna turned away and stared out of the window. "No reason."

"For pity's sake, Anna. You're not still on about that, are you? There is no reason she would have reported me to the General Medical Council. I don't even think she would have known we were together then, had you told her?"

"She saw me kiss you when you and dad visited the abbey," Anna added with a tone of righteousness.

Katherine took a deep breath before responding. "Anna, she's a friend, just a friend."

Anna half rolled her eyes at her. "She is now; she wasn't at the time."

Katherine felt there was no reason in arguing her point further; it wouldn't help. She blamed herself that Anna didn't feel secure in their relationship. It had been important to her that they kept boundaries at the abbey; it was the professional thing to do. She had made sure Margaret had understood that she was in a relationship with Anna, which she said she did. She insisted that she hadn't meant for the card and flowers she'd dropped off to be interpreted that way.

Anna had seemed light-hearted about it when she'd found them on the doorstep the day after they had got back together. When they all began working together in close proximity, Anna's stance had shifted.

Katherine reached out and playfully squeezed Anna's leg. "You know I only have eyes for you." She was determined to try and lighten the mood before the subject could descend into a spat. "So shall I tell you about my plans for Bath?"

Anna smiled and twisted in her seat to face Katherine. "Only if they include a trip to the Jane Austen Centre."

"Of course," Katherine replied, pleased her plan had worked.

"A five-star hotel?"

Katherine looked to Anna and lifted one eyebrow.

"Yeah, okay, silly question. Romantic walks?"

"Guaranteed, we're going to Prior Park."

Anna's eyes widened. "Oh, can we snog on the Palladian Bridge? I've always dreamed of doing that."

"I insist on it." Katherine had plans for the Palladian Bridge, plans that Harry was in on, which was why he'd wished her luck. She was going to propose. Although it was early on in their relationship, Katherine knew she wanted to spend the rest of her life with Anna and there was no better way to show her love and commitment. It also came with the bonus that it would make Anna feel more secure — if she said yes, of course.

They decamped at Abbey House and made their way down to the Royal Oak pub on foot.

The warmth of the pub and the scent of wood smoke hit Anna as soon as she opened the door. It appeared as if a Christmas decoration bomb had exploded inside, as something festive adorned every wall.

"It's lovely in here," Katherine said, having a good look around as she hung up her coat beside the door.

Anna frowned at her. "Have you've never been in?"

"I came once with Becks in the summer, but we sat outside. As a doctor I thought it was best to keep a professional distance from my patients. A village pub is hardly conducive to that."

"Now you have no excuse for not mixing with the locals."

"As long as they don't start displaying their ailments in front of me, I'm sure we'll get along fine."

They were shown to an empty table beside a roaring fire. The double-sided brick-built fireplace was an impressive central feature in the large room, and effectively split the room in two. A long bar ran the length of them both on the far wall. Its low ceilings and dark wooden beams gave it that charm you would expect from a fifteenth-century pub.

As they took their seats, Anna noticed it was the only table without a reserved sign and made a mental note to book if they came again for Sunday lunch. The waitress took their drinks order and left them with the lunch menu.

Katherine perused it. "We really must pop here for lunch one day in the week."

"I'd like that, it beats sandwiches any day."

"But you do make the best sandwiches," Katherine said looking up from the menu.

"This is true. I was once a sandwich artist, you know."

"You jest."

"I do not. When I was at university, I worked in a sandwich bar. My job title was sandwich artist," Anna remarked, a little too proudly.

Katherine shook her head in disbelief. "Well I shall

appreciate my sandwiches even more now I know they are created by an artist. Is it me or is it stifling in here?" She removed her red, Fairisle Christmas jumper to reveal a low-cut top and her impressive cleavage.

"I'm fine, you keep going." Anna winked as she glared at Katherine's alluring chest.

Katherine gave her a boot under the table. "Behave."

The waitress appeared with their drinks, and they gave their order of two roast beef with all the trimmings.

An enthusiastic, overweight, chocolate Labrador appeared beside their table.

"Hello, Moose." Anna stroked his head.

"Moose? Strange name for a dog."

"He belongs to the landlord, Chris." Anna nodded her head in the direction of a rotund, bearded man at the bar.

Katherine grinned "Chris, Moose. Very droll and aptly in season."

"Indeed. He got him to replace his wife."

"Oh, did she die?"

"No, she ran off with the local vicar a few years ago, it was quite the scandal."

Katherine lifted an eyebrow. "I can imagine."

Anna pushed her chair back allowing Moose to get closer to her. He pushed himself against her legs and sat on her foot with a loud harrumph, flopping his head on to her knee.

She ruffled his neck and lowered her head to his. He licked at her face with his long, wet tongue.

"Put him down before he devours you," Katherine said with disgust.

"I just love dogs, don't I Moose? Yes, I do."

Katherine rolled her eyes at Anna's silly voice. "Is this where you declare yourself a dog person and we end our relationship?"

Anna shot a look at Katherine. "I love all animals equally, thank you."

"Well, just don't let Virginia know that."

"As long as she keeps catching those huge spiders around the house, I'll agree to love her more equally than the rest."

"Did you have any pets when you were little?" Katherine asked.

"No, my mum was allergic to most of them."

"That's sad. We always had cats; my mum was the epitome of a mad cat lady. I think it gave her something to focus on other than losing my dad so young."

Anna reached out and rested her hand on Katherine's. "It must have been hard not having your dad around, especially at this time of year. I'm surprised you are such a fan of Christmas."

"It's why I'm such a fan. Every year my aunts, uncles and cousins would rally around us and make a big fuss, obviously it was a distraction technique, but it helped. We all came together at my grandparents' house where we would go for walks; play games; watch television; there wasn't a minute unaccounted for. On Christmas Day I would have a mountain of presents to open from them all."

"That's sweet. It was always just the three of us, until Mum died."

Moose sloped off to his basket by the fire, realising he'd lost Anna's attention.

The door opened and a small group of older ladies entered. They all nodded enthusiastically at Katherine as they took their seats at a nearby table.

"Popular with the younger ladies and the older ladies of Nunswick I see."

Katherine narrowed her eyes at Anna as she took a sip of wine. "They have no doubt heard about my classes."

"I thought with you becoming a trustee you wouldn't have time for that."

"I can't let the pensioners of Nunswick down. Have you not seen the sign-up sheet I put in the tearoom to gauge interest?"

"No, I can't even remember the last time I went in there," Anna replied, biting at her bottom lip.

"Gloria said as much. There is quite some interest mounting. We'll need to organise a regular slot in the barn. I'm thinking ten o'clock most mornings."

Anna licked the foam off her upper lip left by her shandy. "I'm sure we can arrange that."

A figure entered the bar and extracted itself from behind an enormous hat and scarf, revealing Gloria.

"Anna, my darling."

"Her ears must have been burning." Anna whispered to Katherine.

It was clear Gloria was coming in for a hug, Anna stood to receive it. Normally of small stature, Gloria's enormous full length padded coat doubled her size. She wrapped her arms around Anna and pulled her into her, nearly suffocating her.

"I haven't seen you in an age," Gloria said, squeezing her. She noticed Katherine and nodded in her direction.

"Your classes appear to be popular. There's even talk of setting up a Women's Institute group. You've really sprung a bit of life into this village."

Katherine blushed and opened her mouth to speak.

Gloria's attention had moved on and she released a rather red-faced Anna. "Why don't you come in the tearoom anymore?"

"Sorry, Gloria, I don't really pass it anymore," Anna replied, inhaling a deep breath as she spoke. She realised as soon as she said it that it was a lame excuse. Gloria always had time for her, yet Anna hadn't made time to walk down the road to say hello. With an office next to her home and a cafe between them, she was rarely in need of refreshment elsewhere.

"How's your dad getting on?"

"Good thanks. We've just been to see him."

"Well, you give him my love when you see him next. Tell him I'll pop in and see him sometime. I don't forget who my friends are."

Gloria wandered off to the bar and took a seat.

Anna sat back down to see Katherine sniggering behind her hand.

"Did you just receive a telling off from Gloria?"

The sides of Anna's mouth curled down. "If I'm not mistaken, you received a compliment."

Katherine beamed. "I rather think I did."

CHAPTER 3

*A*nna had always loved the idea of having an office in the visitor centre. With its modern, sleek design moulded around part of the abbey's structure, who wouldn't? The sleek design followed through internally with stylish frosted glass-walled offices with a clear glass door. The only disadvantage it held for Anna was watching Margaret at that moment as she marched past with two coffees, one of which she knew was for Katherine.

"Everything okay?" Carrie asked, looking up from her Christmas themed desk. "I'm sure I just heard you hiss."

"Did I?" She had certainly hissed in her head but hadn't intended on vocalising it. "Carrie, how long have you known Margaret?"

Carrie chewed on the end of her pen. "About two years."

"Is she a lesbian?"

Carrie choked on Anna's question and removed the pen from her mouth. "I'm not sure. I've never known her to be with a man — or anyone at all, come to think of it. It's not something we've discussed. She's a very private person. Why?"

"I think she fancies Katherine."

"What makes you think that?" Carrie replied, almost laughing.

Anna regaled Carrie with the tale of the flowers on the doorstep.

"Well, it could be completely innocent as she said. Or not."

"Exactly," Anna replied, only agreeing with the latter part of Carrie's summation.

Carrie pulled her bottom lip up. "I suppose they are closer in age."

Anna glared at her.

"Not that it means anything."

Attempts to distract herself with work for the remainder of the morning fell flat. A welcome sight in the form of Katherine appeared in her doorway at midday.

"Margaret and I are just popping over to the pub for lunch. Shall we go through the branding when I get back? Margaret is heading home after."

Anna's brain took over and responded with a nod on her behalf. Internally her blood was boiling.

Margaret appeared beside Katherine and placed her hand on her shoulder. "Ready, Kat?" She tucked a loose strand of hair from her short grey bob behind her ear.

Katherine winked at Anna. "Won't be long."

Anna let out a loud breath as soon as they were out of sight. "Did you see that?"

"She winked at you! You two are so cute," Carrie replied.

"No, Margaret's, 'Ready, Kat?'" Anna gave an unflattering imitation of their co-worker. "Only Becks and I can call her that."

"Katherine didn't seem to mind."

Anna shot Carrie another look and Carrie winced.

"I didn't mean she enjoyed it, just that she didn't seem to care what she was called."

Anna's stomach rumbled at the thought of food. She fished out her lunchbox from her bag. It hadn't escaped her that she had packed an identical lunch for Katherine that morning which was now going to waste whilst she enjoyed her pub lunch with Margaret and not her.

It also hadn't escaped her notice how Margaret looked at Katherine. She recognised it because it was the same way she knew she looked at Katherine, with a softened expression full of adoration. She was determined to expose Margaret's feelings for Katherine; the only problem standing between her and her goal was that she had absolutely no idea how to.

It felt like hours before Katherine returned. The clock on Anna's desk informed her it was only an hour and fifteen minutes from the time they left to the time Margaret's incessant giggling from down the corridor notified her they were back. As they passed by her desk, Anna scowled at the hand Margaret had placed on Katherine's back. She wanted to shout at her to get off but restrained herself.

A moment later Margaret passed back again and called out, "Bye, girls."

Katherine was only a moment behind as she entered the shared office.

"Hi, Carrie."

"Hi, Katherine. Nice lunch?"

"Lovely, thanks; can't beat scampi and chips. Anna, do you want to come through?" Katherine nodded towards her office.

Anna picked up her laptop from her desk and obediently followed. She pressed the laptop into her stomach to try and cover the sound of the rumble it was making at the thought of scampi and chips. It then did a somersault at the thought of scampi and chips with Katherine. Her lip curled in revulsion as she visualised Margaret enjoying the meal with her.

The trustees' office was tidier and more organised than Anna and Carrie's. It had the Katherine touch about it. There were two desks backed onto each other, like in Anna's own office, and room enough in one corner to allow for a seating area. Two small sofas accompanied a table with an assortment of potted plants centred on it. With colour-coordinating throws and cushions the sofa felt inviting, especially with Katherine and her stockinged legs on it.

Anna glanced at Margaret's desk. It was very clean and minimalist. With other trustees potentially using it, no doubt she had to keep it that way. Margaret was only contracted to work from the office a few days a week, and it was rare to see anyone else. The other trustees were all silent partners in the abbey. It struck Anna that Margaret was in most days now. Did that have anything to do with seeing Katherine more often?

Katherine, on the other hand, completely owned her desk, even though she was supposed to be hot-desking too. She was there for a few hours at least five days a week and so had taken it over. The whole office was so personal to her taste and the style of their house that Anna felt Margaret was intruding in a space that essentially felt like an extension of their home.

Having been schooled by Katherine on how they should behave appropriately at work, Anna sat across from her. The lecture should have been directed at Margaret rather than her. She smiled a bit self-righteously at her thought.

"Something funny, Miss Walker?"

Anna fidgeted in her seat and looked over at Katherine as she put her glasses on. Anna melted at the sight. She'd seen Katherine in her glasses a million times, and it made her weak at the knees every time. If she tied her hair up or crossed her legs, Anna transformed into a quivering wreck. She hoped Katherine wouldn't do that today; they had some serious work to get through, especially now that Katherine had thrown a weekend away into the mix.

"No," Anna replied with a cheeky smile.

"Good, then stop looking at me like you want to eat me up. Let's get on with it, shall we?"

Anna smirked and opened her laptop. "As you wish, boss. Right, branding first. Which did you prefer?"

"Option B. The simple outline of the barn is beautiful, and with Nunswick Abbey Barn in the same font, it complements the abbey branding perfectly."

Anna nodded her agreement. "The only suggestion I have is that we use the brown from A to separate it and give it some distinction from the abbey green. Make it instantly definable."

"That's actually a great idea. I hadn't thought of that."

"I'll go back to the designers and get a final proof for approval by the trustees. We've nearly finalised the leaflet; I just need to get some exterior shots sent over of the barn."

"It's a shame we don't have interiors."

"We'll add them before the season starts for the larger print run. Most of the event attendees are regulars and can use their imaginations. We have the artist's impression too. It will be fine for getting the word out to those coming to the event."

"Fair point," Katherine said, sipping from a mug.

"How many invitations went out to lifetime memberships? I think we need to do something special for them and possibly even include our general members. Maybe give them a gazebo and seating with the trustees at the front to get the best view of the firework display and entertainment."

Katherine flicked through her notebook. "Eighteen in total. Fifteen have confirmed their attendance so far, plus five trustees. I've not counted myself in that. Then there are forty general members confirmed; the other one hundred and twenty-five are general public. So we've more than broken even already; I think we'll hit the two hundred mark in the coming weeks."

"So at least 60 that require special treatment. I'll need you to do some schmoozing. If any of them have a wedding or birthday coming up, I want them booked into the barn. Margaret can help; she seems suitably qualified for a bit of schmoozing."

Katherine lowered her glasses and peered over them at Anna.

Anna drew a line across her lips, and Katherine gave her a nod and a sarcastic smile in return. She wasn't sure why she had to be made to feel like a child for stating the obvious. Perhaps she was being paranoid, overthinking things. No one else seemed to think there was a problem, so maybe if she stopped looking for a problem, she wouldn't see one. Anna twisted her lips. *Unlikely.*

"Anna, are you with me?"

"Sorry?" Anna replied, unaware she had zoned out.

"Am I buying gazebos then? I for one would rather be under some form of shelter."

"Yes. Get two of the larger ones with the walls and windows, and please make sure they are easy to put up. I've completed a risk assessment; we're going to need to install some additional lighting externally, particularly along the pathways."

Katherine scribbled in a notebook. "I'll get right on to it."

"Thanks, it will benefit us all year round if we are going to be holding events outside, so don't scrimp. If we're getting an electrician in, it might be worth getting them to add some power up at the far end of the site too. It might be that we'll need to hire a generator. The band representative is coming tomorrow, so we'll see what they require."

"Understood."

Anna tapped at her keyboard. "Now, the builders will be completely offsite over Christmas, correct?"

"Yes, and they won't return to the site until January second when they will move on to the construction work on this place. They have a separate team they bring in for fitting out interiors, so they will be in the barn from the second too."

"Please reiterate that they don't store any tools onsite over Christmas. I don't want guests tripping on them in the visitor centre when they get their canapés. Speaking of which, the caterers have booked a site visit between Christmas and New Year, just to make sure they bring the correct equipment."

Katherine nodded. "Great, sounds like you have it all in hand."

Anna lifted her eyebrows. "And you'll soon have two projects to oversee; best not tell Becks."

"The projects are planned and overseen by the Project Manager. I just need to check they're following the plan correctly. It's just a shame we'll open the season in March with a building site as a visitor centre."

"When do they aim to start fitting it out?"

"The first week of April. We should be fully operational by the beginning of May."

Anna extracted a tape measure from her pocket and tossed it to Katherine who just barely caught it. "I need to measure up the barn signage, and I need a glamorous assistant."

Katherine smirked. "I'll see if I can find you one."

CHAPTER 4

Katherine walked down the gravel driveway of Abbey House, followed by Virginia a few paces behind. The feel of the gravel under her feet never grew old; she adored the crunching noise it made. It took her back to her family home and walking across their gravel drive with her dad to go to school. It was just another tick in a box when it came to buying the house.

She knew she would come to hate the drive as she grew older and would no doubt struggle to walk on it. It wasn't the best surface for the types of heels she wore to work, today, however, she was strapped into her trusty, leather knee-high boots. The best part of winter was getting to wear them.

Although she was heading to the abbey, it wasn't for work. It was to retrieve something she'd hidden in her desk drawer — an engagement ring. It was safer to have it delivered to the visitor centre where she knew it would reach only her hands. She had fallen in love with it as soon as she had seen it online and feared keeping it at home as she didn't trust herself not to peek at it and get caught by Anna.

She arrived outside the visitor centre and realised Virginia was still close at her heel.

"Wait there for me; you're not allowed in."

Virginia mewed in reply and sniffed at a blade of grass before chewing at it.

She made her way upstairs to her office to find Margaret on the phone; they greeted each other with a smile. Katherine headed straight for her desk and sat.

An initial rummage in the desk didn't bring up the ring. Admittedly it was a large drawer, yet she remembered exactly where she had placed it: at the back, in the centre of a roll of tape covered by a notepad. She pulled the drawer out and began a more frantic search.

It wasn't the cost of the ring that bothered her if it was missing, more so that she needed it now. The thought that there may be a thief in the office didn't sit well with her either.

A deeper search and extraction of most of the drawer's contents led her to the conclusion that any further search was fruitless. It wasn't there. She checked behind the drawers to see if the ring could have fallen down the back. There was nothing more than a few sheets of blank paper, a paper clip, and a ball of fluff.

She sat back and wracked her memory, replaying the ring's placement in the drawer and confirming her movements one by one. There was nowhere else she could have put it; she was sure.

Margaret hung up the phone and beamed at her. "What

a nice surprise, I wasn't expecting you this morning." She got up and walked around to Katherine's desk, perching on the edge of it. "Something up?"

"You could say that." Katherine breathed out heavily.

"Can I get you a cuppa whilst you're here?"

Katherine looked at her watch. They were supposed to be leaving for Bath shortly. She knew she couldn't leave until she'd checked every inch of her desk and she didn't want to alert Margaret to her engagement plans; Anna would never forgive her if Margaret knew before her.

"Tea would be great. Thanks, Margaret."

Margaret gave her a light touch on the shoulder and left the room.

Katherine took the opportunity to scour her desk and filing trays. She couldn't help herself and ransacked the drawer for a third time to no avail. It was gone. She would have to get up early on Saturday morning to find a replacement in Bath or her plans would be scuppered. She'd have to hope Anna wanted a birthday lie-in.

She opened her laptop. A quick check of her emails wouldn't hurt whilst she drank her tea.

Her phone vibrated on the desk. A photograph of Anna cuddling Virginia popped up on the screen. Kat answered the call after allowing herself to admire the warming image for a moment.

"Hey, are you coming? You haven't done something silly like check your emails, have you?"

"No," Katherine replied, closing the lid of her laptop. "I won't be long."

"Is Margaret there?"

She didn't want to lie to Anna, but she didn't want to

feed into her delusions either. "I'm not sure, probably somewhere." It was a half-truth. "I'll be back soon." Katherine hung up her phone.

Margaret appeared with their drinks and placed one on Katherine's coaster with a smile.

"Is she checking up on you? These youngsters can be so impatient these days."

"Mm," was all Katherine could muster in response as she sipped her tea. Margaret was a bit of a dinosaur when it came to the younger generations, but Katherine didn't count her girlfriend amongst them.

"Did you find whatever you were looking for?"

Katherine shook her head and gulped at her tea. She knew she'd have to report its absence to Margaret eventually. She was a little embarrassed to admit she left something so valuable in an office drawer. It would have to wait until after the weekend, however, by which time, she hoped, Anna would be her fiancé.

"Well, I'm sure it will turn up. These things normally do. Usually right where we were looking for them."

Katherine certainly hoped so. She placed her mug down and got up. "I better hurry. Thanks for the tea."

Margaret returned to her desk. "So soon? Well, I hope you have a nice weekend."

"Thanks," Katherine replied as she exited.

Virginia was still waiting for her when she stepped out into the cold air. "Come on, let's get you a big bowl of food ready so you don't starve. Just promise not to eat it all today." Katherine scooped up the cat, tucking her inside her coat. Virginia's purrs reverberated through her chest as she carried her home.

CHAPTER 5

The journey to Bath was a slow one. Why did it feel like everyone else was heading in the same direction whenever you tried to get away? Anna was relieved when she finally spotted a signpost that indicated they were fifteen miles out from the city centre.

"I'm going to give Dad a ring, let him know we're nearly there." Anna fiddled with her phone until the sound of ringing filled the car.

Harry answered immediately. "Happy birthday for tomorrow, love. Katherine has your present from me."

Harry coughed; Anna waited patiently until he had finished.

"Has she? She kept that quiet." Anna glanced at Katherine and received a wink in return. "Thanks, I'm sure I'll love it. We're just coming up to Bath, so I thought I'd check in with you and see how you're doing."

Harry coughed again; Anna's eyes shot to Katherine. She took the hint and waited for him to stop coughing.

"Harry, it's Katherine. How long have you been coughing?"

"Only since this morning, doc. I'm all right."

Katherine twisted her lip. "Have you any other symptoms? High temperature—"

"No, as I keep telling Lucy, I'm fine. She's been fussing at me all morning. I just want to watch the television in peace."

"Well, she is your carer, Harry; she's meant to check in on you. You've got my number. It's your speed dial number two, remember. Call me if anything changes or you feel worse, okay? Promise me."

Harry coughed. "All right, doc, I will. Now you two go and enjoy yourselves."

"We'll ring you tomorrow, Dad, and check on you."

"All right, love, speak then. Don't let me get in the way of your birthday plans."

"You won't, Dad. Now rest up." Anna pressed the end-call button on her phone and tried her best not to worry. "Do you think he's all right?"

"It's hard to tell without examining him; he sounded chipper. A lot of the time this doctoring is about waiting for symptoms to arise to narrow down a diagnosis. It's likely an upper respiratory infection."

Anna wrinkled her face.

"A cold," Katherine replied more plainly.

As Katherine didn't appear overly concerned, Anna put her worries to the back of her mind and gazed out of the window. The countryside had finally given way to beautiful Bath Stone Georgian buildings. "Where to first?" Anna asked, excited to get the weekend started.

"I thought we'd have lunch and head over to the Jane Austen Centre, then nose round the Christmas market after."

Anna's hand stretched out to find Katherine's across the armrest. "Sounds perfect."

The Jane Austen Centre, which turned out to be more of a museum, was just what she had expected, a perfect place for the Jane Austen fanatic. Although more into twentieth-century women writers than nineteenth, Katherine still seemed to appreciate the displays. They both particularly enjoyed looking at the costumes on display, however, they resisted the urge to get dressed up and have their photograph taken; it was far too cold to be removing any layers.

"How does one reach a lady wearing all these clothes, it must take a full ten minutes to extract her from them. How does that work when in the throes of passion?" Katherine asked, puzzled.

"Is this why you prefer twentieth-century literature? The clothing is more convenient for your sexual fantasies."

Katherine nudged at Anna with a smirk. "How rude."

There was no such excuse when it came to trying on a bonnet. Although Katherine protested that it would mess up her hair, she relented when Anna reminded her it was her birthday the following day. With the obligatory selfies taken next to the waxwork of Jane Austen, they moved on to the Christmas market just as the sun was setting.

The city was bustling with people. The bright Christmas lights strung across the streets illuminated the Georgian buildings. A low drone of voices gave way to the echoes of brass bands playing and choirs singing carols as they neared the market. Stilt walkers were doing their best to walk on the cobbled streets and living statues were avoiding the gaze of small children as they pulled faces at them to distract them.

Anna inhaled the scent of chestnuts as they passed a roaster. They made their way through the overcrowded streets, peering over shoulders to make out what was being sold on each stall. Anna was pleased to be able to pick up a couple of extra small gifts for Christmas. She usually just bought Harry a bottle of whisky, but knowing Katherine wanted to make a big deal of their first Christmas as a family, a few extra presents would go down well. She wasn't sure if they allowed alcohol at Baycroft; Harry would no doubt disobey the rule anyway.

Katherine disappeared momentarily putting Anna into a mild panic in the packed market. She shortly reappeared by her side and presented her with a heart shaped lebkuchen. They devoured it between them and washed it down with mulled wine as they watched glass Christmas baubles being blown. Katherine insisted on buying them a set to remember their trip.

After their fun filled and exhausting afternoon, they finally booked themselves in at the hotel. Katherine gave her name at reception and stated that she'd booked a double room. Anna warmed herself by a grand open fire and hoped the staff wouldn't blink an eye that two women were sharing a double. The receptionist handed Katherine a key card with a big smile. They thanked the woman and the porter who had appeared from out of nowhere to scoop up their bags.

They followed him to their room on the top floor.

Katherine had already prepared Anna that it wasn't what she had hoped for. She had tried to book a suite, however, with such a last-minute booking, she was grateful to get any room in any hotel. She hadn't realised Bath was such a popular pre-Christmas destination because of the markets.

The view over the city centre was a beautiful one, with an outlook onto the nearby Bath Abbey and Roman Baths. The room was a good size with all the necessities, including, most importantly, good-quality biscuits and fresh milk in the mini fridge. Katherine was already tucking into the biscuits.

Anna crossed her arms. "I hope you're not eating all the best ones."

Katherine wandered over to Anna and placed a biscuit in her mouth. "Shortbread. Your favourite I believe. Shall we shower and head out to dinner?"

"Have you booked anywhere?" Anna asked through a mouthful of biscuit.

"No, I thought we'd wander and see where we ended up. After seeing how busy it was today, I'm regretting that."

"Well, I'm quite tired, so how about we freshen up, order some room service and a bottle, and watch a movie?"

"If that's what you want, I'm more than happy. Shall we upgrade the shower to a bath for two?"

CHAPTER 6

Katherine woke first the next morning. An instant recollection of the night before reminded her why she lay naked in bed. She had felt quite relieved when Anna had suggested they stay in and order room service, their journey and busy afternoon had exhausted her. She was acutely aware that she might not have as much stamina as Anna and hadn't wished to cramp her style by suggesting they stay in. Their stamina had certainly returned once their steaks and red wine had settled. They had fallen asleep wrapped in each other's arms following a rather heated evening.

Her own plans for the weekend had gradually fallen apart. With Harry unwell, she knew Anna would be distracted and unhappy. What's more, she wondered if the engagement ring going missing might be a sign not to bother, yet she was desperate to ask Anna to marry her. She'd hyped herself up to do it, and she didn't want to back out now.

A lucky spot in the Jane Austen Centre gift shop had at

least resolved one of those problems. Not wishing to hurry Anna, Katherine had wandered into the gift shop to see if there were any gifts she could buy her for Christmas. She had spotted a quaint turquoise ring. The chatty sales assistant informed her it was a replica of one of only three pieces of jewellery that Jane Austen was known to have worn.

It was perfect for a proposal. She could replace it later with a diamond ring or the original, if she could ever find it. The only snag was that the rings were made to order. She had pleaded her case with the assistant, who finally gave in and let her buy the display model. If it didn't fit, they could have it adjusted when they returned home.

Anna was lying naked with the sheets only partially covering her body. Her soft skin called out to be touched. Katherine wasn't ready to wake her yet, so she let her eyes do the touching for her. It took her back to the first night they had shared a bed, the night Harry had fallen. Katherine had woken first, and although Anna was fully clothed then, she had spent about fifteen minutes simply staring at her whilst she slept.

Her heart fluttered at the thought that this beautiful woman might be her fiancée in a few hours. She couldn't hold herself back anymore and leaned forward to kiss Anna's exposed breast, teasing her nipple with her tongue. Her hand quickly found the other one and gave it a light squeeze. Anna's groan told her it had had the desired effect, and she looked up as Anna opened her eyes.

"Happy birthday, my love."

A wide smile crossed Anna's face as she stretched.

Katherine leaned into her and kissed her dry lips. Anna

was always at her most beautiful first thing in the morning. Katherine leaned away, but Anna pulled her back down towards her, allowing her hands to wander.

A knock resounded throughout the room.

"That will be breakfast. Why don't you jump in the shower whilst I sort this?"

Katherine wolf-whistled at Anna's naked body as she leapt from the bed and ran to the bathroom. Katherine grabbed her robe from the chair beside the bed and opened the door to room service. A young man wheeled a trolley in and then retreated with a smile. Her stomach rumbled at the aroma of bacon and eggs.

She laid the table by the window, pouring them both a glass of orange juice. Breakfast was almost perfect; it was just missing two things. Katherine rummaged at the bottom of her suitcase and pulled out two presents, placing them behind the table so Anna wouldn't see them immediately.

She could still hear the shower, so she took the opportunity to call Lucy to check in on Harry. His cough had been playing on her mind. It became more of a concern when Lucy informed her that he'd suffered a choking episode during dinner a few days before. Katherine knew exactly what that meant and had insisted that Lucy call the doctor and ask him to visit that morning.

If it was something like aspiration pneumonia from a piece of food sticking in his lungs, then they should be heading straight home. She decided that would be premature without an update from the doctor first, it would be unforgivable to worry Anna without a diagnosis. Harry wouldn't wish for Anna's birthday, or the prospect of a proposal ruined by him being unwell. They were due back tomorrow; they could go directly to visit him on the way home if need be. It could just be a cold.

Anna emerged from the bathroom wrapped in a white, fluffy robe, with her hair bound up in a towel. She approached Katherine at the breakfast table. "This looks amazing."

Katherine slipped her hand inside Anna's robe. "This feels amazing."

Anna squealed and tapped her arm. "Stop messing about. Let's eat, and then we can get on with the day."

Katherine reluctantly extracted her hand from within the warm gown, and they tucked into a cooked breakfast, croissants, fruit, and cereal.

Anna rubbed at her belly. "I don't think I'll need lunch after all this."

"I thought we'd skip lunch and have afternoon tea at the park instead."

Anna's eyes widened. "Yes, let's do that. It's been an age since I had afternoon tea."

"I called Lucy whilst you were in the shower just to check in on Harry. She mentioned he had a choking episode at dinner the other night."

Anna looked at her with concern. Katherine thought it was best not to elaborate further, she just wanted to make Anna aware in case the worst happened, and it had caused Harry to be ill.

"How was he overnight?"

"He was coughing a lot and was restless, so I've insisted the doctor come to give him the once-over. They'll update us after his visit."

"I'll ring him a bit later then."

Katherine was relieved that Anna didn't seem too concerned, although she was clearly distracted as she finished up her toast. Katherine thought a gift or two might lift her spirits, so she presented her with the smaller one.

"This is from Harry."

Anna shook it and began unwrapping it. "It's my favourite box of chocolates."

"How did I not know you had a favourite box of chocolates?"

"You never asked."

Katherine pulled the sides of her mouth down. Anna had a point. She passed her own present across the table and made a note of the cherry liqueurs as Anna placed them on the table.

Anna unwrapped it eagerly, and her mouth dropped open as it revealed itself — a framed watercolour of the abbey.

"It's lovely, thank you. Oh, look! It's a limited edition, and I have number one."

It had been one of Katherine's first ideas as a trustee to get an artist to paint the abbey. She knew it would go down well in the abbey shop.

"You've really spoilt me with this trip and a beautiful present. I'm not sure I deserve it."

"You do, and more," Katherine replied, running her foot up Anna's bare leg.

"There's more?"

"There might be, no promises."

After a few hours of shopping, interspersed with selfies

taken at every tourist attraction from Pulteney Bridge to the Roman Baths, they collapsed into the car.

"Can we go via the Royal Crescent?" Anna pleaded.

"Via! It's on the opposite side of the city to the park."

"Don't make me say it's my birthday."

Katherine grinned. "Oh, all right. If I'd have known you were going to be this difficult, I would have left you at home."

After what amounted to a thirty-minute detour, twenty minutes of which were spent sitting in traffic, trying to cross back to the other side of Bath, they hit the outskirts of the city and arrived at Prior Park. Katherine noted it may have been quicker to walk. She was glad they hadn't, it was a steep climb out of the city, and she would have been too exhausted to have appreciated the park. They strapped their boots and coats on and headed to the tearoom.

Breakfast was now feeling a long time ago; either that or it was her nerves building up. It had only just crossed her mind that Anna might say no to her proposal. She pushed those thoughts down and tried instead to think positively. Anna might say no, but she didn't believe she would.

Halfway through what turned out to be a rather delicious afternoon tea, Katherine took herself off to the ladies to have a quiet word with herself. She faced the mirror and took some deep, slow breaths. She hadn't accounted for getting this nervous and hoped it didn't show. Her hands were sweaty and shaky; she rinsed them under the tap to cool them down. Feeling calmer, she rejoined Anna who appeared to be bathing in her hot chocolate. Katherine reached over and wiped a smear of cream from her nose with a grin.

"This has to be up there with my top birthdays."

"What was your best?" Katherine asked, already feeling nervous again just being with Anna.

"Hot air balloon over Luxor," Anna replied immediately through a mouthful of miniature chocolate log.

Katherine blinked. She was a little jealous; travelling was something she very much hoped to do with Anna one day, once the abbey was self-sufficient.

"Wow, you could have told me I was competing with that. I don't think I would have bothered trying."

"That's why I didn't tell you." Anna winked. "Right, I'm stuffed. Shall we walk this off, slowly? I'm dying to get a selfie on the bridge."

Katherine was less eager to get to the bridge so quickly, but Anna's enthusiasm lifted her spirits.

They walked down the hill towards the limestone Palladian Bridge, admiring its reflection in the water. It really was something, one of only a handful in the world.

Anna was overwhelmed and rushed ahead, up the low steps. Katherine followed, taking a slower approach towards the historic structure. She admired her beautiful girlfriend as she moved enthusiastically around the bridge, hunting for eighteenth-century graffiti and touching the stone, no doubt to listen to the voices it had absorbed.

Katherine rested herself on the balustrade between two central Ionic columns and admired the moulded architraves. She had a newfound appreciation and respect for them since restoring her own at Abbey House.

Anna continued to wander, taking shot after shot on her phone. Katherine couldn't help smiling at the love and passion Anna had for anything old. She turned and leaned on the balustrade, peering over to admire the water as it trickled over the weir below; it soothed her nerves. A touch to her pocket told her the ring was safe.

Anna eventually rejoined Katherine, pushing her cheek against hers to take a selfie.

It was now or never.

She reached into her pocket and extracted the ring, loosely hooking it on to her finger.

She turned to face Anna. "Anna."

"Yes?" Anna replied, her face still beaming.

Katherine took Anna's free hand that wasn't clamped around her beloved phone. Anna instantly smiled in response.

"Will you…"

Anna's phone rang.

"Oh, that might be the doctor." Though she gave Katherine a crumpled look of apology, Anna answered the phone and walked down the bridge away from her.

"Marry me?" Katherine let out with a sigh to the vacant space in front of her. Her disappointment was short-lived and swiftly replaced with concern when Anna turned to look at her with panic in her eyes. She met her at the bottom of the bridge.

"Please talk to Katherine — she's here."

Katherine gave her a questioning frown.

"It's Dad. They've taken him to hospital."

Katherine took the phone from her. "This is Dr Atkinson." It was the first time in a while she had referred to herself as such, and she had to admit it was a strange feeling.

"Yes, yes, mmm, yes. Okay. I understand. We'll be there as soon as we can." She hung up and passed the phone to Anna.

"What's wrong with him?"

"Aspiration pneumonia," Katherine replied, almost choking on the words. "Come, we better go home." Katherine walked back up the hill to the car park with Anna at her heels.

"Pneumonia, that's serious," Anna said between panted breaths.

Katherine stopped and turned to face her. "It can be, yes." She had hoped not to have this conversation, not on Anna's birthday. "Parkinson's patients can have more difficulty than others with swallowing. If they choke, particles of food can get lodged in their airways, which leads to pneumonia." She took Anna's hand. "Pneumonia in anyone is very serious and—"

Anna nodded. "Dad's not just anyone; he has Parkinson's."

"Exactly," Katherine said, pulling her into a hug. The wind caught Anna's hair and swept it across Katherine's face. She lifted her hand to move it and realised she still had the engagement ring hooked on her finger. She slipped it back in her pocket, along with her proposal and an excessive amount of disappointment.

They arrived back at the hotel to be greeted by champagne and flowers in their room. Anna was shocked by their appearance, Katherine less so. She'd ordered them in anticipation of an engagement. Anna was too distracted to disagree with Katherine's suggestion that they must have been placed in their room by mistake. Within ten minutes, they had checked out and were on their way to the hospital.

CHAPTER 7

The journey home was a sullen one. Katherine decided it would be best if she drove; she said Anna would be far too distracted to be behind the wheel. Anna wasn't sure how she felt; she didn't feel distracted. Numbness was about all she could pinpoint. She knew the shock would subside and hit her eventually. She wondered if that was what Katherine was waiting for; she didn't want her driving when it did.

They had exchanged very few words since they'd left Bath, and they were almost at the halfway point home. Both, it seemed, were deep in their thoughts. Anna glanced sideways at Katherine. Maybe she was in shock; maybe that was why she was quiet — although she hadn't seemed overly surprised by Harry's diagnosis.

Was she angry they had cut their weekend short? It had been Katherine's suggestion they leave right away. Anna felt disappointed to leave early too. It had been their first time away together, her birthday, and her first time in

Bath. Her head spun with escalating thoughts. She couldn't stand the silence anymore.

"I'm sorry that the weekend hasn't worked out how you planned. I really enjoyed what time we did have together."

Katherine pulled her lips straight. "Never mind, we have all the time in the world for weekends away. Being there for Harry is what's important now."

"You were about to say something on the bridge."

"It was nothing. It doesn't matter now."

Something told Anna it did matter. She didn't feel comfortable pushing the point further in case it caused upset. If Katherine wanted to elaborate, she would have.

"Are you okay?" Anna asked, not wanting the conversation to end when it had only just started.

"Yes, I'm just worried about Harry."

Anna stretched her legs out and yawned. "How did Lucy not pick up that it was pneumonia?"

"She's not a doctor, and Harry only presented with a cough initially. She followed protocol and checked his temperature. Elderly patients don't always have a fever, their symptoms tend to be more subtle. They might be unsteady and lack an appetite like other pneumonia patients. As we know, these can be day-to-day symptoms of Parkinson's for Harry."

Anna propped her elbow on the car door and rested her head in her hand. "We didn't get our snog on the bridge."

Katherine's initial smile quickly slipped away. "No, no, we didn't. I guess it will just be the three of us for Christmas too."

Anna's head shot round to look at Katherine. "You think he'll be in the hospital until then?"

"He'll be extremely lucky to still be in the hospital then."

Anna chewed at her bottom lip. She knew what Katherine was insinuating; she didn't want to say outright that there was a possibility Harry wouldn't make it. Anna wasn't sure how to react. The old Anna probably would have had palpitations followed by a panic attack, but she wasn't so quick to hit panic mode anymore. She'd been through this before and felt more equipped to deal with it calmly. Harry hadn't been well for a while, and she knew he wouldn't live forever. It hurt nonetheless to think of life without him. She pushed the thoughts away; they weren't helpful.

It felt all too familiar arriving at the hospital; at least this time she wasn't in an ambulance breathing into a paper bag. They were directed to the geriatric ward. Katherine led the way, her hand firmly held by Anna. Although they had arrived during visiting hours, they were shown into a waiting area and told a nurse would be with them shortly.

A moment of quiet reflection mixed with the familiarity of the hospital smell hit Anna, and she felt a rush of emotion finally come over her. She closed her eyes to prevent the tears she could feel forming from falling. They broke through the barrier anyway; she felt their warmth as they rolled down her cheeks. Katherine noticed her distress and wrapped her arms around her, attempting to soothe her with gentle strokes of her hair and kisses against the side of her head.

It was at least ten minutes before a nurse entered. They parted as the nurse approached but their hands found each other.

"Which one of you is Mr Walker's daughter?" The nurse's eyes flitted between the two of them as if making an educated guess as to who was the more likely candidate.

"I am," Anna said, stepping forward a little. "This is Dr Atkinson, my partner."

The nurse gave Katherine a smile and nod of acknowledgement.

"How is he?" Anna asked, trying to move past the formalities.

"He's stable; he was a little restless when he came in, so we've given him something to help him sleep. We've got him on intravenous antibiotics. It's too early to tell how he is responding. We'll have a better idea tomorrow after some blood work. Would you like to come through? Probably best just one of you for now if you don't mind."

Anna twitched her face at Katherine. A squeeze of her hand from Katherine gave her the courage to follow the nurse from the waiting room.

Anna entered the stuffy hospital ward behind the nurse and immediately began removing some layers of clothing. The nurse directed her to the bed nearest the window. Anna preferred window beds; at least she knew Harry would get some idea if it was night or day when he woke. It was so easy to get disorientated in hospital as to what day it was, let alone the time of day.

Harry was asleep as the nurse had said. Anna took a seat beside him and held his hand. She hated seeing the needle in the back of it. His elderly skin was so thin and fragile, she knew it would leave a nasty bruise. His sallow complexion drew her attention to his face. Where there would be colour in his cheeks, they now appeared pale. The hospital gown made him appear weak and vulnerable. She hadn't quite appreciated how much he'd aged in recent months.

She took in the ward whilst she sat. It was festively decorated with red tinsel wrapped around the metal headboards and a line taped along the nurses station. A heavily decorated Christmas tree stood in one corner of the room, every branch had something hanging from it causing it to droop. It looked rather sad and was a stark contrast to Katherine's elegant minimalist creation at home.

It reminded her of the Christmas trees from when she was a child. Her mum had acquired quite a collection of hanging ornaments over the years and insisted there was room on the tree for all of them.

It was a wonder the nurses found time to add these little touches to the ward. It certainly brightened the place up and they were no doubt appreciated by the patients.

Conscious that Katherine was waiting, she only stayed for ten minutes. The nurse reassured her he was unlikely to wake anytime soon and encouraged her to return tomorrow. Anna left and walked straight into Katherine's waiting arms outside the ward.

"How did he look?" Katherine asked, placing an arm around Anna's waist.

"He was asleep; so, you know, peaceful. At least he

wasn't covered in bruises this time. He had a couple of drips in him."

Katherine nodded. "All necessary. I've been thinking: you should take a couple of days off."

"Why?" Anna snapped. She was startled by her own tone of voice, but the idea of being away from the office and leaving Katherine unguarded with Margaret on the prowl didn't appeal to her.

Katherine twitched her head at the question. "So you can be here for Harry of course."

"I've far too much work to do. I can only visit Dad during visiting hours after work anyway."

"Well, take some time for yourself then; this is a big shock to your system."

"I'll be fine. I don't want to be away from the office. Having work as a distraction will do me good."

Katherine placed her hands on her hips. "Why don't you want to be away from the office?"

Anna twisted her lips. She knew any answer would annoy Katherine, so she remained quiet.

"Anna, is this about Margaret again?"

"No," Anna lied unconvincingly.

Katherine raised her eyebrows in reply and walked away.

Anna followed a pace behind, regretful that she had said anything. She didn't need Katherine angry with her now when she needed her the most. As if she could read Anna's thoughts, Katherine stopped and reached back. Anna quickened her pace and took her hand.

CHAPTER 8

Katherine entered her office and placed her mug of peppermint tea down on her coaster. It always made her smile; it had been a gift from Anna on her first day as trustee. It was printed with a Virginia Woolf quote: *In case you ever foolishly forget, I am never not thinking of you.*

She needed something to make her smile. She hadn't quite shaken her disappointment from the failed proposal; her sadness for Anna that her birthday weekend was interrupted by the news of Harry being ill; and that Christmas wouldn't be what she had planned.

Any happiness from a successful proposal would have been short-lived in light of Harry's diagnosis, so it felt right that she hadn't asked her. Anna had refused to take any time off and denied that it had anything to do with Margaret. Katherine couldn't understand what Anna was seeing that made her think Margaret was interested in her.

She had at least persuaded Anna to leave earlier in the afternoons. It was for purely selfish reasons. If Anna drove to the hospital in daylight, then she would only worry about her driving in the dark once a day on her return. The narrow roads of the Nunswick Valley were not for the faint-hearted at any time of the day. If it snowed over Christmas, as the weather reports were suggesting, she would insist on accompanying Anna on every visit.

They had fallen into a routine at home with Katherine having dinner ready for Anna on her return. She had previously invoked a no-work rule at the house, which Anna had always respected. Now that her workload had increased, Katherine could see that not being able to attend to work responsibilities was causing her stress. She'd relented, although she needed to manage her own workload it wasn't up to her to dictate terms to Anna.

Although Anna's blood pressure had improved since Harry had gone into Baycroft, Katherine continued to monitor her. Anna had agreed that if Katherine suspected her body wasn't dealing so well with the stress, she would slow down. Katherine made a mental note to increase her checks now that Harry was back in the hospital.

A proof copy of the new leaflet stared up at her from her desk. Anna must have placed it there before she left for the hospital. A Post-it note was stuck to the front, written on it in Anna's appalling handwriting was a poem: *Check me, correct me, don't forget me! x* Although the poem could use some work, the leaflet was certainly impressive. A brief scan immediately highlighted two typos. Anna had known Katherine was the woman for the job and she was going to need her special pack of highlighters for this.

Her mobile phone vibrated on the desk and made her jump.

"Hey, Becks. Are you okay?" Katherine asked, rummaging in her drawer whilst trying to balance the phone to her ear.

"I'm good, how are things with you? How's Harry?"

Katherine extracted a box from the drawer and stared at the fifteen highlighters with a twinkle in her eye. "He seems to be responding to the antibiotics, so that's a good sign." She looked down to close the drawer when something unexpected caught her eye. The missing ring box was staring straight back at her.

"That man is as strong as an ox."

"Mm," Katherine replied, lifting the box out and opening it. Relief swept over her as the diamond ring twinkled back at her.

"You still there?"

"Sorry, I've just found something I thought I'd lost. What were you saying?" Katherine tried to focus her mind. "Oh, Harry. Well, I'm not happy with myself regarding him. I should have spotted that he was very unwell. I should have done something more when Lucy told me he'd had a choking episode. I knew what it meant; that's why I insisted on the doctor."

"You knew what it could mean, not that it did mean that. It sounds like you did everything possible."

"Not really; I was going to check what vocal therapy he was having. He was very monotonal last time we visited, and I was so distracted making sure everything was perfect for her birthday and the propo—" Katherine stopped herself. She hadn't even told Rebecca about the proposal; she didn't want anyone's opinions on it, be them positive or negative. She wanted to follow her heart.

"Even if you had checked and they weren't doing any therapy, whatever treatment they started wouldn't have made a difference in that space of time," Rebecca replied.

Katherine let out a silent sigh of relief that she hadn't picked up on what she nearly said.

Rebecca continued. "He would have still choked. Please don't over-analyse this and try to find a way to blame... yourself — wait a minute, what did you just say?"

"Nothing?" Katherine replied through gritted teeth. It was nigh on impossible to slip anything past Rebecca.

"You bloody did! Were you going to say 'proposal'? Did you propose in Bath? I can't believe you weren't going to tell me."

"If I may squeeze in a word or two..."

"Sorry, got a little carried away in the excitement. So?"

"Yes, I was going to propose, but as I was about to, the doctor rang."

"Oh, Kat, my heart is breaking for you."

Katherine scratched at her scalp. "It's fine. I'm fine with it."

"You sure do sound fine." Rebecca laughed and then squealed. "I'm so proud of how far you've come. So, are you going to ask her again, or not again since you haven't asked yet?"

Katherine rolled her eyes. "I don't know. Everything is a little awkward at the moment what with Harry and her obsession that Margaret has the hots for me. I didn't realise she had such a jealous streak; it's very unattractive."

"Margaret? As in the trustee, your boss of sorts? Scandalous."

"We're just good friends," Katherine replied, fanning herself with the leaflet.

"I'm sure you'll sort it out between you — if you communicate."

"Chance would be a fine thing; she has a huge workload what with this New Year event. She's up early and straight into work, and then with a hospital visit she's back late, eats dinner, works, and then hits the bedroom exhausted."

"Oh, are we a little frustrated?"

Katherine stood and opened a window. "This has nothing to do with that, thank you. I'm just worried about her. Even if Margaret was interested in me, which I know she isn't after a rather embarrassing conversation some months ago, it's not like I encourage her. I think Anna's just seeing things that aren't there."

"All I can suggest is that you look at every interaction you have in future through Anna's eyes. See what she is seeing."

Katherine hummed her agreement and checked her watch. "I've got to go, Becks; I have to sign off the building works with the project manager."

"Exciting."

"You're telling me! They finished a week earlier than planned, which gives me a bit of breathing space before Christmas and the guys an extra week's holiday, which they are chuffed about."

"I'll see you next week then. Send my love to Anna and tell her I hope Harry gets well soon. I'm sorry not to see him on Christmas Day even if he did call me... what was it?" Rebecca chuckled.

"A big, scary barrister lady. Well, you are. See you soon."

Rebecca signed off with the sound of a kiss being blown down the phone.

Katherine examined the small box on her desk and checked inside again, still unable to believe the ring had just been lying in the drawer. Either it had been there all along and she had simply missed it, or someone had taken it, thought better of it, and returned it. It was probably best not to mention it to Margaret if it had been taken; the person had returned it after all. If they realised they had made a mistake, she didn't want to ruin someone's career over it.

Now she had two rings and no idea what she was doing with regards to the proposal. Everything had become a bit strained since Harry went into hospital. She was trying hard not to act out of the ordinary around Anna even though she felt guilty for not having gone straight to Harry the morning of Anna's birthday. If she was honest about it, there was scope for having turned the car around the instant she heard him coughing.

She tried to focus on Rebecca's words and not blame herself: Harry wasn't Katherine's patient or medical responsibility anymore. The feeling of guilt rose in her once more; he was more than a patient now, he felt like a father to her. Having lost her own when she was young, she'd never had a replacement figure until Harry. She knew it would be difficult to raise the subject with Anna, especially while Harry was ill. Katherine didn't want to look as if she was trying to steal her anguish, though she did want to let her know she wasn't alone in her pain. Whether Anna would understand that, she was unsure.

Katherine put the box into her pocket; she would have to find somewhere safe at home to keep it. Taking the high-vis vest from the back of her chair and the hard hat from the seating area table, she headed out to the barn, clipboard in hand.

Mark, the project manager, greeted her outside what would be a fire exit for the three-hundred-year-old barn. Anyone who wasn't part of the building team required escorting onsite. Katherine inhaled as she entered; she couldn't get enough of the timber scent.

She made a quick scan to make sure any developments carried out since she had last visited were coming along as they should be. It was beginning to come together now that the windows were in. A whole row of them had been placed into the new timbers on the side of the barn that faced the abbey. It made a cracking view. The concrete floor had set perfectly over the underfloor heating, and all the electrics were in place. The centralised doors were just being manoeuvred into place with the assistance of two large tripod lights, as the winter sun was setting faster than the building team could work.

Mark led her through the open-plan event room, which accounted for 80 percent of the barn. She looked up at the exposed beams as she passed under them — another thing she couldn't get enough of; it was a beautiful space.

They reached the far end wall, which had been constructed within the barn to house a kitchen, toilet facilities, and two offices, all of which she was pleased to see had been plastered. She followed Mark down a corridor and into the office that had been earmarked for the marketing and events manager. It was small yet adequate.

Both offices had external doors that led directly onto the grounds in case they needed access when the barn was in use. That way they could work unhindered whilst retaining access to the facilities. Mark flicked on a light as they entered. Katherine jolted in surprise; not only did she not expect the electrics to work yet, but she had been relying on the loss of sunlight to expedite the meeting. It now appeared she was in it for the long haul. As she took a seat at the fold-out table that appeared to be Mark's desk she noticed some strange shapes in the concrete floor. They were cat paw prints. That certainly explained the grey marks that had appeared on the kitchen floor a few weeks before.

CHAPTER 9

s Christmas Eve fell on a Friday, it seemed everyone had treated it as any other Friday and come into work. Anna particularly had a lot of work to finish up, partly because most of the suppliers for the New Year's Eve event were closed over Christmas.

She had made a point of phoning them all to go over arrival times and confirm their requirements for the site. The signage company wouldn't be installing the barn signs until the morning of the event, which was adding to her stress level. She checked and rechecked the quotes to make sure everything was correct.

Her hand instinctively reached into the tub of chocolates that sat between the desks but withdrew as she found the bottom of it. She picked it up and investigated it. There was only a handful left, none of which she liked. She never understood why coconut had anything to do with chocolate; they just didn't work together.

She looked over to Carrie. "Please tell me you ate most of these."

"Sadly not," Carrie replied without even looking up.

Anna watched a grin spread across her face. "Why are you even here today? Don't you have the arms of a loving family waiting for you at home?"

Carrie looked up and pulled her lips to one side. "The boys are home from university, and neither of them thought to bring their televisions home."

"Oh, dear." Anna knew exactly what that meant.

"Hmmm. I've had to create them a rota, a rota for two grown men to share our television so they can play their PlayStations without arguing. I have never been more pleased to be at work on Christmas Eve."

Anna couldn't contain her laughter, and despite Carrie's seriousness, even she had to join in at the ridiculousness of it.

"What are you still doing here?" Carrie asked. "Are you not seeing your dad today?"

"I'm waiting for the gazebos to be delivered before I head off."

Anna clicked refresh on the tracking website to see how far away the driver was. It was parcel 220 of 350 to be delivered that day. How anyone delivered 350 parcels in a day she would never know. It said they were currently delivering parcel 215 of 350.

She'd made a mental note for future events that non-perishables should be delivered within two weeks of the event date and to never arrange an event for New Year again. Although she had organised many events, she hadn't appreciated that the countryside was a little different. She could get anything she wanted in the city in an instant.

If she was to keep the job, future events would, she hoped, be less stressful. She wouldn't be organising them around a building site for a start, whilst trying to advertise said building site to the event attendees.

With gazebos finally delivered and checked, she took the delivery note to Katherine to reconcile her purchases. She stood at the threshold of the office and watched as Margaret leaned over Katherine's desk to point at the laptop screen. With her other hand resting on the back of Katherine's chair, it created the effect of Margaret thrusting her breasts in Katherine's face.

Anna coughed and Margaret pulled herself upright, taking a step back. That confirmed to Anna that she knew exactly what she was doing. Someone guilty of nothing wouldn't have moved.

"Anna." Margaret flashed her a shocked smile and retreated to her desk.

"Margaret," Anna replied in as flat a tone as she could summon. She approached Katherine's desk and resumed Margaret's position, placing the delivery note on her laptop. "I'm heading off to the hospital."

"I thought you weren't going since you have to go in tomorrow morning?"

"I have to collect the barn leaflets from the printer, so I'll pop in on him."

Anna popped a kiss on Katherine's cheek; she could feel the smile it created on her lips. She knew it was against the rules, and it also felt a little like she was marking her territory in front of Margaret, but she didn't care.

"I'll see you later, *Kat*," Anna said with a smirk as she passed Margaret. "Bye, Margaret."

"Bye," Margaret replied with a flat smile.

Anna left the visitor centre with a wide grin on her face, pleased to have put Margaret on the back foot.

The traffic in town was horrendous. Everyone, it seemed, was doing last-minute Christmas shopping. A diversion to the printers before they shut for the Christmas period hadn't helped, but she needed to get her hands on the leaflets. She didn't want to leave them to the peril of a courier between Christmas and New Year. She was exhausted and irritable by the time her tyres hit the gravel outside Abbey House.

"How was Harry today?" Katherine asked as Anna collapsed at the kitchen island.

"Asleep again. They said I should wake him as he was asking for me; I just can't bring myself to when he looks so peaceful. Can you pass me some scissors please? I need to check these leaflets."

Katherine pulled some scissors from the drawer and handed them to Anna, watching as she nervously opened the box.

Anna took two leaflets out and passed one to Katherine. If they weren't right, there was nothing to be done about it now.

"They look perfect, well done."

"Thanks," Anna replied, pleased that someone had

acknowledged the work that had gone into it. "You know *she* hasn't said anything to me about the leaflet."

"Who?"

"Margaret."

"Well, she's not directly your boss anymore; we agreed I would take marketing and events under my wing."

"It's not just the leaflet; she barely speaks to me at all unless I address her directly. It's like she's pretending I don't exist."

"I think you're reading too much into it."

Anna raised her eyebrows. "She's always touching you."

"She's a touchy person," Katherine replied casually as she wiped the work surface.

"No, she isn't! She literally isn't." Anna could feel her anger rising at Katherine's naivety. Was it even naivety? If Katherine and Margaret did have something between them, wouldn't she be saying the exact same things to throw her off the scent? "Have you never noticed she touches you and only you? She was practically thrusting her breasts in your face earlier."

Katherine laughed. "You are being ridiculous, and jealousy is not an attractive quality. I know it's likely coming from insecurity, but I'm with you. I love you. What are you not understanding? Margaret is just a friend. Please give this notion up."

Anna shook her head. "I can't believe you don't see it."

"Anna! She is not a threat to our relationship. In fact, I'd say the only threat at this moment is you, not her." Katherine's tone had changed from sympathetic to angry and she glared at Anna from across the island.

Anna blinked in disbelief that Katherine was now twisting it back onto her, as if she were responsible for this disagreement. Feeling under attack, Anna decided to attack back.

"Whilst we're airing things, something struck me: Lucy isn't a doctor, but you are. You knew that morning that he'd had a choking episode and what it could mean. Why didn't you tell me?"

Anna knew instantly she'd hit a chord with Katherine from the silence that followed.

"I didn't want to worry you unnecessarily. I insisted the doctor visit as soon as I knew," Katherine finally replied, calmly.

"He's my dad, Katherine, not yours. I had a right to know. I don't need protecting, for pity's sake; I need facts so I can ensure *my* dad receives the right care."

Katherine inhaled sharply. "I'm sorry." She rubbed her hand along Anna's upper arm. She shrugged it off.

Her heart pounded in her chest. Had she gone too far? She couldn't take it back now, and she had meant every word of it. Not having been there for her mum when she had needed her, Anna had become determined to do everything she could for her dad. The very person who was supposed to be supporting her do that had been standing in her way preventing it.

The guilt she had felt when her mum had died was something she didn't intend to feel again. It had overwhelmed her. She'd always taken for granted that her parents were okay, going happily about their lives in Nunswick. By the time she had realised that wasn't true, it was too late. In all the times she thought back to why she hadn't visited more regularly, she could think of no-good reason. Life with Jessica had simply taken over. Now there was no Jessica and no mum, and no going back.

Not one for confrontation, Anna felt the need to get away from the situation before it escalated further.

"I'm going to bed."

"What about dinner?"

"I'm not hungry." That was a lie; she was starving. She'd just lost her appetite.

"Anna."

She retreated from the kitchen, ignoring Katherine's pleas, and made her way to the shower. She couldn't turn around because Katherine would see the tears in her eyes, and that wouldn't help the situation. Continuing to talk whilst she was angry was something she had learnt not to do from previous experience.

An early night was in order anyway; tomorrow was going to be a long day. The hospital had requested visitors come before twelve so they could have a Christmas party in the ward with lunch. Anna thought it might also be to do with not wanting drunk relatives turning up late in the afternoon on Christmas Day.

With Rebecca at the house all day and overnight, it was going to be exhausting. Although Anna and Rebecca had become closer during the occasional weekend visits she made to Abbey House, Anna still didn't feel like one of the "gang".

She had hoped to spend some quality time watching movies with Harry whilst Katherine and Rebecca nattered in the kitchen. She loved watching Harry's face light up during his favourite part of a movie and listening to his narration over a part he thought could be improved upon. Now she was going to be part of the gang whether she liked it or not. No doubt Katherine had filled Rebecca in on Anna's thoughts on Margaret and convinced her Anna was being ridiculous, as she'd put it.

If Katherine didn't see Margaret's behaviour as a problem, then Anna would have to deal with her on her own. She knew this would mean confronting her and it was not something she was looking forward to — it might mean risking her job. She just couldn't sit back any longer and watch Margaret making her moves on Katherine. If Margaret was a man making moves like that, he wouldn't have a job. It was morally right to address it directly and sensible to wait until the new year.

CHAPTER 10

Katherine woke the next morning to find Anna was already up. Another one of her hopes for Christmas Day dashed — waking up beside Anna. Realising the time and that she'd forgotten to set her alarm, she wrapped her dressing gown around her. Anna's was still on the back of the bedroom door; she must have dressed already.

She found Anna sitting at the kitchen island with a cup of coffee, engrossed in her laptop. Resisting the urge to make a dig about working on Christmas morning, she opted for a simpler greeting. "Merry Christmas."

"Merry Christmas," Anna replied as she continued to stare at her laptop.

Katherine reheated the kettle and turned the oven on.

"Can I get you anything?"

"I'm fine, thanks."

She felt foolish for hoping that normality would be restored after Anna had slept on it. She was clearly still angry.

"The weather is forecasting heavy rain. You'll drive safely, won't you?"

Anna closed her laptop and looked up at Katherine as if sensing her concern. "Of course. I'm going to head off. Becks will be here soon, won't she?"

"Yes."

Anna nodded and gave her a weak smile before leaving the kitchen.

Katherine made herself a cup of peppermint tea to curb the stress she could feel building in the pit of her stomach. The kitchen was eerily silent; being alone on Christmas morning was another thing she hadn't planned.

Her phone vibrated; it was Rebecca. Noting the time on her phone, Katherine hoped she was ringing to say she'd be a little bit late. It would give her time to have a bath and hopefully reset herself.

"Hey," Katherine greeted her, unable to muster much more enthusiasm.

"You okay?" Rebecca asked with a tone of concern.

"Not really. I'm having a crap Christmas."

"It's hardly begun. I fear I'm about to make it worse; I'm not coming. I'm so sorry. I've been up all night with a very unhappy stomach. That will teach me to go on a blind date to a seafood restaurant on Christmas Eve."

Katherine clamped her eyelids together to control the overwhelming urge to cry. It was no use; nothing could hold them back, and tears erupted.

"Shit, please tell me you're crying because of your crap Christmas and not me."

Rebecca waited patiently for Katherine to calm herself.

"It's everything — and you."

"Sorry, Kat. You know I'd be there with you if I could. You have Anna. You can have a cosy Christmas, just the two of you."

Katherine cried some more, raiding the tissue box in front of her to mop up.

"What have I said now?"

"We argued last night. She accused me of keeping the seriousness of Harry's condition from her."

"Well, you kind of did that but you did it…."

"For the right reason. I know, and we've been here before. I apologised, then she shrugged me off and went to bed without dinner. She couldn't even stand to eat with me."

"Where is she now?"

"At the hospital." Katherine opened her dressing gown and wafted it to cool herself.

"In this weather? I don't know about Nunswick, but it's snowing heavily here. It's all over the news about it being a white Christmas."

Katherine looked out of the window and burst into tears again. The one thing she couldn't control to make it a perfect Christmas was the snow, yet it was the only thing that had worked out.

"I'm sorry, I don't know why I feel so emotional at the moment."

"It's all right to get emotional occasionally; Christmas hasn't turned out how you expected."

Katherine felt that to be true.

"I was so looking forward to it after last year alone."

"You said it was fine if I went skiing," Rebecca replied indignantly.

"I lied; it wasn't. I was miserable. All I wanted was for this Christmas to be perfect, with everyone I love around me."

"Stop, you're going to make me cry in a minute. Did you fight about Margaret again?"

"She's fixated, Becks." Katherine sniffed. "She accused Margaret of shoving her breasts in my face."

"Was she? Did you do what I said and look at it from Anna's angle?"

Katherine thought for a moment and shook her head. "I don't know, maybe she was. Have I got this all wrong?"

"I don't know, but you need to calmly talk it through with Anna when she returns and listen to her. Whether or not Margaret is hitting on you is beside the point. Anna thinks she is, so you're going to have to deal with it or you'll seem like you're just belittling her thoughts. If you haven't already, go and put your face on and then have a glass of champers to calm yourself down. Perhaps get the turkey in the oven if you haven't already. Whoops, sorry, the thought of food has set me off. I'll call you later."

As she hung up, Katherine felt Christmas was barely worth bothering with. A bath brought no improvement to her mood. Preparing lunch provided some distraction, especially with the assistance of an insistent Virginia. She sat on the island and mewed instructions at Katherine.

"Yes, I know, Virginia." She didn't know at all. She never knew what Virginia was mewing at her, but her reply always seemed to quieten the cat. She'd seen Helena do it so many times in the past. They would hold what appeared to be private conversations between them, more often when Helena was cooking. They joked that Virginia had been a famous chef in a past life and was simply giving instructions on how best to compile a dish.

Virginia had been closer to Helena than herself and felt her absence immediately. She would search the house for her, mewing in hope of a response. Katherine would find her sleeping in places where Helena's scent was strongest, like her side of the bed or her favourite chair.

Things came to a head during Katherine's darkest days following Helena's death when she could no longer stand the sound of the cat reminding her that Helena was gone — she locked Virginia out of the house. It was something she came to regret almost immediately when she realised Virginia was all she had left of Helena. She spent two days searching for her to no avail and had almost given up ever seeing her again when she heard the cat flap click one morning. The relief she had felt was overwhelming, it was as if part of Helena had returned.

Virginia stopped mewing for Helena, and with some extra attention from Katherine, the cat eventually returned to her old self. Where she would sit on Helena's lap in the evening, she would sit on Katherine's. They had come to an understanding that although they both missed Helena, they needed each other to get through it.

Katherine felt a twinge of sadness at Helena's absence and wiped a tear from her eye. She tickled Virginia under the chin and then poured herself a glass of champagne. She usually had a rule of no champagne before twelve; today was different, she needed one now.

The sound of gravel crunching caught her attention, and she raced to the door, hoping to see that Anna had returned. She wasn't expecting anyone and was hardly in the mood to entertain, so she was particularly deflated upon opening the door to discover Margaret standing on her front step.

"Merry Christmas!" Margaret exclaimed.

"Margaret, what an unexpected pleasure," Katherine replied monotonically. "Merry Christmas."

"I couldn't help overhear that Anna would be with her father this morning. I thought I'd just pop round and give you your present, make sure you weren't lonely."

Katherine's stomach lurched. "Present? I didn't realise we were doing presents. I haven't got you anything"

"I don't give to receive, Katherine." Margaret beamed at her.

Katherine held the door open, she felt she had no choice but to invite her in. She took Margaret's long black coat and gestured for her to go through to the kitchen.

"What a beautiful house you have. And so exquisitely decorated."

As they entered the kitchen, she realised the bottle of champagne was on the island next to her full glass; she'd have to offer Margaret a glass. A check of her watch told her that Anna was likely to be back soon. If she found Margaret there, all hell would break loose. The only solution was to get rid of her as soon as possible.

"Champagne?"

Margaret's eyes sparkled. "Yes, please."

Katherine poured half a glass and passed it to her, hoping she would drink it quickly and leave. They clinked glasses, toasting to Christmas. Katherine took a couple of large gulps in the hope it would make Margaret do the same.

It didn't; she took a small sip and placed the glass back down on the worktop. Katherine made a mental note to wash the glass before Anna saw it, then realised how ridiculous her thoughts were. She was a woman entertaining a friend in her own home; she had nothing to hide.

Margaret extracted a gift from her bag and passed it to Katherine. "It's just a little something."

Katherine removed a large red ribbon and unwrapped the shiny gold paper. Her cheeks blushed with embarrassment that she had nothing to give in return. She groaned internally when she realised it was a long jewellery box. Things were about to get more awkward. Opening it revealed a necklace, as she had suspected — a rather beautiful necklace at that. A gold chain with a pearl pendant lay on the silk insert.

"Margaret, I can't possibly accept this. It's too much."

"Of course you can." Margaret insisted, lightly tapping Katherine's hand. "It's just a little token of my appreciation for all your hard work since joining us at the abbey. You've lightened my load and made each day a little brighter."

"That's very kind of you, Margaret, but I think it's too much."

"Nonsense. Here, let me help you with it."

Before she could argue, Margaret had taken the necklace out of the box and placed it around Katherine's neck. She locked the clasp in place and then returned to face Katherine.

"There, stunning," Margaret said, lining up the pearl with Katherine's cleavage and patting at it.

Katherine felt uncomfortable at Margaret's proximity and took a step backwards. "I must just check lunch."

"Of course."

Katherine placed the necklace box on the work surface and attended to the turkey. It was almost ready to come out.

Margaret wandered over to the sliding doors with her champagne glass. "I hadn't quite appreciated the view you have of the abbey."

"It's even better from upstairs."

"Oh, really?" Margaret turned and walked back to Katherine.

Katherine instantly regretted the way she'd phrased her sentence.

As Margaret drained her champagne glass, Katherine saw an opportunity to get her out. "I'd offer you another, but I expect you won't want one as you're driving, and to be honest, Margaret, I've rather a lot to do getting lunch ready. No doubt you have places to be so don't let me hold you up."

Katherine placed a hand behind Margaret and gestured to the door.

Margaret's face was awash with disappointment. "Yes, of course."

"Thank you so much for the necklace. It really wasn't necessary," Katherine added as she ushered her across the hallway.

As she closed the front door, Katherine realised she had closed it on the only person who had made the effort to see her on Christmas Day. Then, wracked with guilt over her thought, she poured herself another glass of champagne.

Harry and Rebecca couldn't help being unwell, and Anna would be back soon. Wouldn't she?

As she washed up the champagne glass, she realised how much Margaret's visit had unnerved her. What did she expect her to do with the necklace? Surely she realised Anna would ask where it had come from. Was that her intention in giving it to her? She could pretend it was an old one; Anna didn't exactly have a photographic memory of her entire jewellery collection. Yet she didn't trust Margaret not to drop her in it by asking why she didn't wear it, or, if she did wear it, making everyone aware that she had bought it.

Was she overthinking it? She was beginning to sound like Anna. If it was a gift given to her by a friend, why would any of it matter? Katherine was beginning to feel that it hadn't been given in such an innocent manner. The way Margaret had patted it on her chest had been uncomfortable. Perhaps Anna had been right all along.

She tried to recall conversations she's had with Margaret and the interactions they'd shared. Margaret was always in close proximity and quite hands-on at times — well at every opportunity really if she was being honest, they could well have been flirtations. She couldn't recall one time when she'd seen Margaret behave this way with anyone else in the office, despite having said as much to Anna. She'd just assumed she was like that with everyone.

A rush of warmth swept through her as she realised Margaret could very well have feelings for her. In desperate need of some fresh air, she opened the back door. Virginia shot out from under the garden table and ran past her into the kitchen, seemingly unimpressed by the snow that was now falling heavily.

Another check of her watch made her draw in a sharp breath. Her heart raced suddenly making her cough. Where the hell was Anna? She picked up her phone and called her, now determined to tell her about Margaret's visit. She was met with the sound of Anna's voicemail. Tears found their way to her eyes again. After all her expectations for Christmas, the only thing she wanted now was to wrap her arms around Anna and never let her go.

CHAPTER 11

*H*aving gone to bed early the night before, Anna had woken early on Christmas morning. Still angry about their argument, she had resisted the urge to pounce on Katherine when she woke as planned. Instead, she lay beside her and watched her sleep.

She thought Katherine would always be on her side and was disappointed that she wasn't when it came to Margaret. There didn't seem to be a way to make Katherine see things from her point of view.

Even so, it had been difficult to leave her alone to go to the hospital. Christmas wasn't going the way Katherine had planned, and Anna knew the disappointment she must be feeling. At least Rebecca would be along soon after she left. She would be able to understand the situation better than most and offer Katherine useful solutions.

Harry was asleep again when she arrived at his bed. She'd barely exchanged more than a few words with him since he'd been admitted. The nurses seemed pleased with his progress, however, and said he had been holding brief, albeit confused, conversations with them. She could have done with his chirpy attitude this morning, telling her everything would be all right as she knew he would.

She opened the Christmas card she had hurriedly written for him that morning and placed it beside his bed. With an eBook waiting to be finished on her phone, she leaned back into the hospital chair and began reading. She felt in no rush to get home. They wouldn't be able to resolve their issues with Rebecca around. The rest of the day would involve them skipping around each other whilst trying not to let on to Rebecca they were having issues, both knowing full well that Rebecca was aware of the issue because Katherine would have already talked it over with her. Anna sighed and tried to focus on her book. Why did relationships have to be so complicated?

The arrival of various visitors to the other patients on the ward made her look up from her phone from time to time. They were laden with gifts, reminding Anna that she hadn't given Katherine her present before she left. At one point she realised she'd dozed off.

"That you, love?" Harry asked softly.

Anna grabbed his hand and lightly squeezed it. "Yes, it's me, Dad. Are you all right?"

"Did she ask you?"

"Did who ask what, Dad?" Anna questioned, unable to make out what he was saying.

"Bath. Did you say yes?"

Anna frowned and leaned in closer. "What did you say, Dad?"

He was asleep again. She resisted the urge to shake him awake and ask him to repeat what he'd said. Had he been dreaming? Did who ask her what? Did he mean Katherine was going to ask her something in Bath? What would Katherine ask her that her dad would expect her to say yes to?

Anna shot bolt upright. The bridge flashed into her mind. Katherine was about to ask her something when the phone rang. Then there had been flowers and champagne in the room on their return. It was all starting to make sense. Had Katherine been trying to propose on the bridge? Her heart pulsed in her chest, almost choking her. How could she have been so stupid?

Anna's mind raced. If Katherine had planned to propose, why hadn't she since? They had spent little time together since Harry went into the hospital. Was Katherine giving her some breathing space whilst so much was going on? Or had she changed her mind? Anna's hand shot to her mouth, and she closed her eyes. All this time she'd been obsessed with Margaret, and Katherine had been wanting to ask her to marry her. *You bloody idiot, Anna!*

No wonder Katherine was so insistent that Margaret was just a friend. She couldn't see what Margaret was doing because, despite Margaret's efforts, Katherine wasn't looking at her; she was looking at Anna. She'd never had a reason to be jealous, and now she wouldn't be surprised if her actions had pushed Katherine right into Margaret's arms.

If Katherine wasn't going to ask her to marry her, then Anna was going to ask her instead. There was no better time to do so than during the fireworks at New Year's Eve, first, there was a lot of making up to do to ensure Katherine said yes.

CHAPTER 12

Katherine paced the kitchen, grabbing a handful of tissues from the box on the island each time she passed it. The turkey had been left to cool on the side, and the vegetables, all prepared, were either on the stove, in water, or in the fridge. As she passed again, she took a large swig of champagne. A silly mistake, she knew it would only make her more emotional.

The sound of gravel alerted her to a car. She wanted to race to the front door, instead she held herself back. She'd already been disappointed once today. In a moment of panic, she envisaged it was the police arriving to give her bad news. She closed her eyes, hoping to clear her irrational thoughts. An image of the police visiting her in her hospital bed with the news of Helena's death appeared instead.

Katherine lifted her head and gasped for a breath as she struggled to control her escalating thoughts. The relief she felt when she heard the key in the lock was overwhelming. The pounding of her heart pulsated through her entire body, making her light-headed. She reached out for a nearby stool to sit on before her legs gave way.

"Kat!" Anna called from the entrance hall.

Katherine could hear her, but the adrenaline rushing around her body fogged her head and seemed to prevent her from speaking. More tears fell from her puffed eyes.

Anna appeared at the kitchen door and dropped her bag. She ran to Katherine, wrapping her arms around her. "What's the matter?"

Katherine rested her head against Anna's chest and sobbed. It took a few minutes until she could find her voice. "I was so worried. I didn't know where you were, and the snow is so heavy. I tried calling, but it went to voicemail. Did you turn your phone off to avoid me?"

Anna's eyebrows shot up, and she lightly pushed Katherine's chin up to make eye contact. "No, of course not. I forgot to charge it last night, and then I was reading at the hospital; it probably killed my battery." Anna reached into her pocket and extracted her phone. The black screen told them she was right. She wiped away the tears from under Katherine's eyes. "Sorry, I should have checked it. I assumed you'd be too busy with lunch and Becks to be thinking about me. I'm sorry if I worried you, and I'm sorry about the whole Margaret situation. I don't know what I was thinking. I trust you completely. It was stupid of me to be jealous."

"I'm sorry, too, for not telling you the whole story about Harry. I didn't want to ruin your birthday before it had begun."

"I shouldn't have said what I did about him not being

your dad. I know you love him, too, and not having one of your own, you probably see him as a dad. It was mean of me."

Katherine nodded through her tears. "I do love him, and I feel terrible that I didn't turn the car around as soon as we heard him cough. I can't imagine him not being in our lives, Anna."

"I know, and hindsight is a wonderful thing. Please don't beat yourself up about it." Anna looked around the kitchen. "Wait. Where is Becks?"

"She rang after you left to say she was ill."

"You've been alone all morning?" Her face crumpled. "Oh, Kat. You should have messaged me straight away. I would have come back sooner."

Katherine knew it was time to fess up "Well, I haven't been alone the whole time. Margaret popped in briefly." Katherine looked up at Anna to gauge her reaction.

Anna took a step back and then walked over to the kitchen sink. "What did she want?"

Katherine took a tissue and wiped her face. "She overheard that you would be with Harry for the morning. She brought me a gift, a necklace."

Katherine watched Anna as she washed her hands in the large butler sink in silence. Unsure whether she should continue or not, she was relieved when Anna finally broke the silence.

"Go, on."

"She freaked me out a little if I'm honest. I think you may have been right about her having a thing for me. I tried to refuse it, then she insisted on putting it on me — things got a little creepy. At one point I think she was hoping I'd show her the view from our bedroom. I ushered her out after that."

Anna dried her hands on a tea towel and returned to Katherine's side.

"Wow, that does indeed sound a little creepy."

Katherine wiped her eyes again. "I'm going to deal with it, both her and the necklace. I promise you. I just need to be careful how. I have another little mystery to solve too."

"Are you going to elaborate?"

"I promise I will tell you once I solved it. You need to focus on Harry. Trust me, I've got this. Okay?"

Katherine knew if she revealed anything about the ring going missing it would spoil her proposal. She was relieved when she felt Anna take her hand and squeeze it.

"Okay. I trust you." Anna flashed her a reassuring smile and then lifted the champagne bottle to examine it. "I think I better finish this; I'll get a glass."

Relief swept through her with Anna's words of trust, if somewhat momentarily, something still niggled her. Katherine wasn't exactly convinced she had 'got it'. Anna may be on to something about Margaret's feelings for her, could she also be on to something regarding the General Medical Council? Margaret would certainly have a motive and it had worked in her favour by splitting them up, albeit briefly. At the time she had only met Margaret a handful of times. Would that have been enough for Margaret to have developed feelings for her and plot to destroy her relationship with Anna?

What lengths would the woman go to now, considering they were in a serious relationship right under her nose?

Was she capable of taking the ring from her drawer? Its disappearance almost put a spanner in her engagement plans and gave Margaret more time to work on Katherine. Thinking back to when she had made enquiries on the phone to the jewellers and then purchased it, Margaret had entered their office moments after. She had also mentioned to the jeweller the date she needed it by. Margaret could have been eavesdropping nearby and then put two-and-two together.

She felt sick to think of all the times she believed Margaret was being friendly when instead she may have been trying to coerce her into something. All the while Anna was watching and perhaps thinking she was complicit. She would need to concoct a plan, one that would allow Margaret to admit her guilt freely. Margaret was not the kind of woman you wanted to back into a corner.

Another wave of emotion swept over her as Anna returned to her side with a glass. She felt foolish. Foolish for being taken in by Margaret and foolish for not trusting Anna's instincts. Those same instincts appeared to tell Anna that Katherine needed a hug at that point. She collapsed into her open arms as her eyes yielded yet more tears.

"Don't cry, everything is okay. I'm here."

Katherine composed herself and pulled away. "I don't know what's wrong with me."

"You've let your thoughts run away with you and your disappointment overwhelm you, that's all. You need to relax." Anna looked around the kitchen. "Shall we eat later? I'm only hungry for one thing right now." She placed her hands on either side of Katherine's face and gently wiped the moisture from under her eyes. She placed a soft kiss on each cheek and then a firm kiss on Katherine's waiting lips.

Katherine felt herself weaken at Anna's touch and was grateful she was still sitting on the stool. Her legs widened and her dress rode up as Anna pushed herself into her, bringing their bodies together as close as she could. It left an open invitation which Anna took as her roaming hands worked their way up Katherine's thighs as if drawn to the warmth of a fire.

Katherine writhed and leaned back as Anna's fingers found their destination. She arched her body back as Anna's lips found her neck and kissed it.

"Shall we take this somewhere more comfortable?" Anna whispered in her ear.

A nod was all Katherine could muster as Anna withdrew her fingers.

They tore at each other's clothing as they climbed the stairs, eager to get them off. Both were completely naked by the time Katherine fell back onto the bed, ready for Anna to finish what she started.

The bed was empty when Katherine woke except for a sleeping Virginia tucked into her side. Her mind felt clearer — and her body relaxed, finally — after some attention from Anna. She stretched, much to the annoyance of Virginia, who got up and tucked herself against Anna's pillow.

"Traitor."

Virginia yawned in response.

Anna appeared in the doorway with a mug. "I was just coming to wake you. I thought you might like a cup of peppermint tea."

"Thank you," Katherine replied, reaching out for it. She was gasping for a drink after their activities.

"I've put lunch" — Anna sat beside Katherine and looked at her watch — "early dinner on. We'll have to reheat what turkey we need."

"Sorry, I was supposed to be making lunch."

"It's fine. I can cook, you know."

"I know."

"Is it present time yet?" Anna asked, pulling a present wrapped in brown paper from her back pocket and presenting it to Katherine.

"Thanks. Festively wrapped, I see. I'd forgotten all about presents. Mine hadn't even made it as far as the tree." Katherine opened her bedside table and extracted a small, square, flat present. "This one is from Virginia."

At the sound of her name, the cat got up and climbed onto Anna's lap.

"Well done on the wrapping, Virginia."

Virginia mewed, rubbed the side of her head against the wrapping paper, and then returned to her spot by Anna's pillow.

"I think she wants you to hurry up and open it."

"She's almost as bossy as you," Anna replied, tearing at the paper.

Katherine winked at her. "Almost."

"A Jane Austen coaster. Oh, Virginia, you shouldn't have."

"You said you wanted a new coaster by the bed. Virginia must have overheard."

"And come with us to Bath." Anna chuckled as she leaned forward and placed a kiss on Katherine's cheek. "Thank you, I love it."

"That's not your main present."

Katherine reached around under the bed, her naked bottom poked out from under the duvet and presented itself to Anna.

Anna kissed it. "Again? You're insatiable."

Katherine laughed between grunts as she extracted a large present from under the bed.

"Here." Katherine let out a lung full of air as she heaved it onto the bed.

"Golly, thank you. Open yours first."

Katherine tucked the duvet back over herself and then tore into the small, long present. It had a familiarity to it that sent her heart racing. The removal of the wrapping paper revealed a jewellery box. It was from the same jewellers as Margaret's gift. What if it was the same one? She didn't want Anna's gift to be tied to the memory of Margaret's. Opening the box revealed a delicate gold chain with a diamond pendant attached; her relief was audible.

Katherine lifted it out. "It's beautiful, thank you and nothing like Margaret's gift."

"Good. The woman clearly shares my fine taste for women, but I would hope that is where our similarities end."

"You are taking this all very well, I'm not sure I would

if someone had been trying it on with you."

Anna twisted her lips. "Well, I trust you and I'm excited about our future together. What else matters?"

Katherine smiled and placed her hand on Anna's. It was exactly what she needed to hear. "Open yours, be careful — they are fragile."

Anna peeled the sides of her present down, revealing an old hardback set of Jane Austen books. She examined the top one and then turned the rest to look at the spines. Her jaw dropped as she looked to Katherine.

"I can't accept these."

"You can and you will. They aren't first editions or anything. I thought they looked like a nice set from the early twentieth century. That time when all the best female authors were about."

Anna lightly tweaked one of Katherine's nipples, which had appeared over the duvet. "How dare you! There is no one better than Jane Austen."

Katherine pulled the duvet around her with a grin. "Debatable, another time perhaps."

"To be honest, I wasn't expecting anything. Having a birthday just before Christmas is the worst. It was always one birthday and Christmas present."

"Doesn't that mean you get something bigger and better?"

"In your case you've spoilt me on both occasions."

Katherine brushed a few strands of Anna's long, brown hair behind her ear. "You deserve it. Why don't you come back to bed?"

"Why don't you get up?" Anna leapt back and yanked the duvet off Katherine. "On second thought, I don't mind soggy sprouts." Anna crawled back across the bed to Katherine's naked body and kissed her soft belly.

"No, but I do." Katherine pushed Anna back, causing her to flop onto her side of the bed. Virginia managed to vacate it in time and ran for the door.

"You tease," Anna replied as Katherine clambered clear off the bed.

Katherine disappeared into the en-suite. "Yep, that's me. I'll be down in five."

Anna had been right; she could indeed cook. The roast potatoes were perfection; the sprouts were a little overdone for Katherine's liking, but Anna had managed to reheat the turkey without drying it out. Katherine thought it best not to dampen her achievements by mentioning she had forgotten to make some bread sauce.

After their late-lunch-cum-early-dinner, they cuddled up on the sofa, determined to watch a war film in honour of Harry. They settled instead for a television series set during the war and much more suited to their taste, especially as there was mention online of a lesbian character. They just had to hold out hope she would survive to the end of the series.

Katherine's thoughts drifted to Anna and marriage. She now, more than ever, wanted to ask Anna, and she was determined not to mess it up again. It would need to be planned properly with minimal chance of interruption. She twisted her lips as a thought sprang into her mind. Perhaps a certain interruption would enhance a proposal, like some New Year's fireworks. Katherine grinned to herself and kissed Anna's head. Her chest tingled as she felt Anna's arm tighten around her in response.

CHAPTER 13

*N*ew Year's Eve came around far too soon for Anna's liking. The first few days following Christmas they had taken some refreshing morning walks and after visiting Harry they curled up in front of the fire with Jane Austen and Radclyffe Hall.

The tranquillity of those days was soon a distant memory as the new year moved ever closer and the work-life balance shifted firmly back into the work camp. She had spent a few hours working early in the mornings when Katherine was still asleep, and the site visit by the caterers had required their attention for a few hours one afternoon.

Any distraction, be it work or play, was most welcome. Since she had had the idea of proposing at the New Year's Eve event, her body had been freaking out with butterflies, sweats, and a racing pulse. It didn't seem sure if it was excited or nervous. She almost reached for her pills at one point to settle herself, but her brain told her she was excited. It was annoying how her body always reacted in the same way to both emotions.

She had contemplated nipping off to a jeweller on one of her visits to Harry, but Katherine always came with her. In the end, she gave up the idea. She knew she would want to get a ring, too, so it would be better if they chose together, assuming Katherine said yes.

Visits to Harry came with the risk that he may mention Katherine's proposal again, and in her presence. However, he was often dozing or too delirious to make much sense when he did speak, something Katherine had reassured her was normal in people fighting infections. As Harry's condition improved, Anna had to catch him up with the situation and her plan whilst Katherine had nipped to the toilet. He could barely contain his smile when she returned. It took some quick improvisation on Anna's part to convince Katherine that she had just told him a joke.

The sign company were due onsite early, so Anna had gone ahead to deal with them, leaving Katherine at home. She was relying on her to be in top form that evening, so she thought it best to let her get up at her own pace. It had been a shock to see Katherine in such a state of worry on Christmas Day. Her usually strong facade seemed to have fallen, and she felt she'd had a glimpse of what Katherine had been like after the accident and before Rebecca rebuilt her.

Anna didn't like what she saw, it was scary. Katherine was her rock, she looked up to her as someone older, wiser, and solid. It was a strange realisation that everyone is just about holding things together in their own way and sometimes the mask slips.

She knew she was going to have to step up for Katherine, not be so complacent that she was okay. Part of her began to worry that perhaps it would be too much to propose. It wasn't as if Katherine had asked her, what if she'd had second thoughts?

At least they were finally on the same page when it came to Margaret, although neither of them had any proof other than a weird feeling. She was like a dark cloud hanging over their heads. They hadn't discussed it further since Christmas Day. Katherine said she would resolve it and she was in the best position to do so. She knew wading into the situation herself would only make it worse, and let Margaret know they were on to her.

There was just enough time to grab a cup of peppermint tea before a van pulled into the car park. She pushed the feeling of guilt away that she still hadn't been in to see Gloria. She greeted the two chaps who were installing the signage and set them about their work with a promise of coffee to follow.

They had settled on laser-engraved wooden signage. It would be a more natural fit with the site, and the outline sketch of the barn would work well in that style. They had ordered a very large slice of wood to go in the ground. The top section had a laser engraving of the barn logo and underneath the name "Abbey Barn" with an arrow pointing along the path. Once in place, the earth would be built up around it and a rockery added to help support it and cover the concrete base.

The sign for the barn itself was more subtle. A smaller wooden slice was engraved in the same way, without the arrow, and was to be hung from an ornate, wrought-iron bracket seated on the corner of the barn.

She gave the two workers an hour before taking some coffee to them. The crunch of snow underfoot told her it would be well received. It reminded her she would need to wear her thermals when she changed later for the event.

Clipboard in hand, ready for a site walk, she arrived just in time to see the sign standing and the rockery nearing completion. The frozen ground had given way when faced with two determined men with spades. A couple of well-placed solar-powered lights would ensure it was well lit.

She hoped the trustees would be impressed when they saw it that evening. She knew most of the trustees were on her side; Katherine had said as much. She just needed to impress them one final time to seal the deal on the job. Not that it would be the worst thing in the world if she went back to her tour supervisor position; they had a couple of great tour guides returning for the season. However, her work over the past month had cemented her passion and determination to return to her roots. She wasn't sure how she would handle watching someone else do what she saw as her job, or if she'd even be able to stay at the abbey to watch.

The abbey staff were due to arrive at seven o'clock when the caterers did; their own cafe staff would be assisting them and running the bars. Until then it was down to her — and Katherine, when she arrived — to get the site ready. The band would arrive at five to set up their gear and would then disappear until ten. Anna was then hoping to get home for a bath, a change of clothes, and some food. Although the buffet supplied by the caterers looked delightful, she couldn't be sure she'd have five minutes to eat any of it.

Guests weren't due onsite until nine. She hoped they would have enough to entertain them until the fireworks at midnight, after which she planned for them to disperse. She'd hired a magician to do a walkabout to keep the guests amused and an artist to draw caricatures.

She heard the front door of Abbey House closing. The delightful naked-lady knocker always gave a loud clunk when it was closed. Katherine crossed the drive and entered the abbey gate. Their eyes locked as Katherine approached Anna, and their lips widened at sight of each other. Their hands found each other seconds before their lips.

"The signage is looking great. I love the engraving." Katherine ran her fingers along the grooves, then stood back and admired it. "You can't miss it either."

"I'm just going to do a run-through. Can you sanity check me?"

"Of course, I am at your disposal."

Anna turned in the direction of the carpark. "Right, everyone arriving by car will be met and directed by Carrie and the tour guides. They will need to clear some of the snow from the carpark before people arrive. Once the carpark is full, they will spill over into the village. The tour guides said they will come early to clear and salt the carpark and paths for us."

"Great, one less job for us!" Katherine replied with relief.

Anna walked Katherine through the abbey site to the

far end, running through every minute detail and checking for health and safety issues.

"We'll need to set the gazebos up for the members and trustee VIP tent here and we'll need to lay out a serving area for the bar and buffet inside." Anna turned away from Katherine and pointed as she spoke. She soon realised she had lost Katherine's attention as a snowball hit her firmly on the back.

"Oh, it's like that is it?" Anna bent down to scoop up some snow. A snowball flew over her head just missing her. She turned quickly and threw a snowball at Katherine, a scream told her she'd hit her target and she scooped up more.

"That got me in the face." Katherine spat as she wiped her face.

Anna was quick off the mark again as she managed to catch Katherine off guard, throwing another at her body.

"Okay, okay, you win," Katherine shouted, raising her hands. "I should have known better than to pick a fight with you."

Anna approached her and kissed her. "Yes, you should know better." She smirked as she dropped a snowball on the top of Katherine's head.

"Unfair! I'd surrendered. You're a dirty player."

Anna held her hands up. "Okay, let's call it quits before we exhaust ourselves, we have a lot to do."

They arrived back at the carpark with a long list of additional jobs scribbled on the bottom of Anna's already long list.

"Carrie's parking team will have Abbey Barn leaflets to hand out once everyone is onsite. Can you find some membership forms to go with them? I think they are in the cupboard in your office. Leave them by the entrance with some high-vis jackets."

"Of course, Miss Walker. Is there anything else you require?" Katherine asked playfully.

Anna's phone rang; she extracted it from her coat pocket. "Hold that thought, it's the hospital." Anna shoved the clipboard at Katherine. She hadn't been expecting a call from them and hesitated before she answered it.

Katherine took her hand and squeezed it. "It's okay — we'll deal with it — whatever it is, together."

After a few moments of silence she gave Katherine a thumbs up. Katherine wrapped her arm around Anna's shoulder and squeezed her; Anna noticed her subtly wipe away a tear as she did.

"He's going home," Anna sang out as she hung up. "The nurse said he still has a long recovery ahead of him, and there's no reason he can't be cared for at Baycroft. They are releasing him tomorrow morning."

Anna felt sick with relief that he was well enough to go home. She just had to get through a long night before she could visit him. Hopefully she could take him some news to cheer him up — that was, if her courage didn't completely abandon her before the fireworks went off.

CHAPTER 14

Katherine watched Anna as she pulled on her thermals.

Noticing, Anna posed suggestively.

She gave Anna a wink. "Hot! They would look better on the floor, though."

Anna's face creased and blushed. She picked up her trousers to whip her with but missed as Katherine leapt out of the way and disappeared into the dressing room.

By the time Katherine reappeared following two outfit changes, Anna was dressed and heading for the bedroom door.

Katherine's phone vibrated on her bedside table.

"It's Becks. I'll catch up with you."

Anna nodded and pecked her on the cheek. "Don't forget to take some of the Abbey Barn leaflets from Carrie at the gate before you head up to the VIP tent. Sell, sell, sell."

Katherine answered the phone whilst blowing a kiss at

Anna as she left the bedroom. "Hey, Becks. How are you feeling?"

"Better thanks. I thought I'd ring and wish you both good luck for tonight."

"Thanks, I'm sure we won't need it; Anna seems to have it all in hand."

"No doubt." Rebecca chuckled. "How was Christmas? Sorry again to ditch you like that."

"It was up and down. I let myself get wound up into a state when Anna was late getting back from the hospital. I thought it was happening all over again."

"It's okay to glitch occasionally, especially during stressful times."

"Anna said I'd let everything overwhelm me," Katherine replied, sitting on the bed.

"You were pretty excited about your Christmas plans and they kind of crashed around your ears. How do you feel now?"

"Better. Nervous about tonight."

"I thought you said it was all under control."

"The event is yes. Margaret on the other hand —."

"Oh, do tell. Has she finally declared her undying love for you?"

Katherine could hear Rebecca stifle a giggle. "It's not funny, Becks. It's all rather awkward. She turned up on Christmas morning with a gift, an expensive gift at that. It all got a little weird and creepy."

"Anna was right all along then?"

"It's looking that way. I also believe she might have stolen an engagement ring I bought for Anna; it reappeared later, but still. I'm also thinking it might have been her that informed the GMC about us. I'm going to confront her about it tonight."

"Wow, it's all happening in Nunswick. You've told Anna all this I assume?"

"Yes, of course, apart from the engagement ring, it would have given the game away."

"Be sure before you confront Margaret. You can't come back from accusing someone of being a thief. Technically you can't even accuse her of being a thief since it was returned, it's called taking without owner consent. Record her on your phone if you're looking to get evidence."

"Good idea, I hadn't thought of that. I better go. Anna will be waiting for me."

"One thing before you go: any news on that proposal?"

Katherine grinned. "I'm going to ask her tonight during the fireworks."

"Romantic."

Katherine hung up with Rebecca's well wishes and on the promise she would ring back tomorrow with news of the event and proposal. She extracted the rings from the back of her underwear drawer and placed them in the inside pocket of her long coat — along with Margaret's necklace.

By the time she arrived onsite, the first visitors were already arriving. Anna must have already briefed Carrie about the leaflets as she held a bundle out to Katherine as she passed. She found Margaret in the VIP tent and split the bundle with her. She needn't have because Margaret spent the entire time glued to her side. This did bring the advantage that Margaret could introduce her to the trustees she hadn't yet met in person and some of the more important abbey members.

Two such people were a local couple, Gerald and Susan, who were silent trustees. From what Katherine could gather they seemed to have an unhealthy obsession with caravanning, which was why she hadn't yet met them. After their chat, Margaret advised her against attending any party they invited her to. She had once made the mistake of going to one of their summer parties only to find out they were nudists.

For all her potential faults, Margaret was good company and had been a good friend. It was regrettable the way things had turned out. Katherine had hoped she had misinterpreted Margaret's behaviour on Christmas Day due to her emotional state. The little touches and level of attention she gave Katherine throughout the evening told her she hadn't misinterpreted anything; Margaret was clearly being flirtatious. She seemed almost possessive of her, occasionally clinging on to her arm. Now her eyes were finally open it was blindingly obvious the woman had feelings for her.

During a moment of respite from her clingy colleague, Katherine managed to take a breather outside the gazebo. Due to the cold weather, Anna had decided to put four walls on the gazebos and with all the bodies crowded in there it was starting to resemble an oven.

Katherine drank in the busy site for the first time since everyone's arrival. It was jam packed with young families and groups of friends, no doubt exchanging stories of their Christmas and making promises to meet up in the new year. A large group were even dancing around the band on a make-shift stage. Everyone certainly seemed to be enjoying themselves.

She felt a sense of pride in Anna for pulling off a remarkable job, but then Anna was a remarkable woman, she'd expect no less from her. Katherine smiled at her thought and checked her pocket for the rings. They were safe. Now it was just a matter of getting one on Anna's finger.

A figure appeared through the darkness, illuminated only at their feet by the lights on the path. There was a familiarity to the walk that Katherine recognised.

"Anna, is that you?" Katherine called out.

"Yes, can you help me with these trays?"

Katherine stepped forward to meet her on the path and took a tray of canapés from her.

"How's it all going?"

"I'm exhausted; I haven't stopped."

Katherine looked at her watch. "Not much longer now. How's it going over at the visitor centre?"

"Great. There's a constant stream of people coming to the bar and to stock up on food, which I'm hearing great things about. The caricature artist has a long line of people waiting. Before I left, the magician had stepped in to entertain them, I think he's trying to warm up before coming back out here."

"Who can blame him." Katherine laughed.

They took the canapés into the gazebo and placed them on the fold out tables beside the bar. Anna cleared up the empty trays, straightened the tablecloths and gave the bar a quick stock check.

"I better get back; I've got a list of jobs before the fireworks are set off." Anna turned to leave.

"Anna."

Anna stopped and looked at Katherine. "Yes?"

Katherine placed her hands on Anna's shoulders and looked her in the eye. "Breathe. You're doing a great job. I'll come find you at midnight."

A smile washed over Anna's face, and she rushed from the gazebo in a frazzled blur with the empty trays.

As the evening drew closer to midnight, Katherine knew she couldn't put off confronting Margaret much longer. She didn't have a lot of confidence in the only plan she'd managed to come up with. The first part, to get her tipsy, Margaret had managed herself much to Katherine's relief. The second, to seduce her into a confession, was now down to Katherine. If Margaret thought she might get somewhere with Katherine, then she might be looser lipped. She knew she'd have to play the seductress carefully. She unbuttoned her coat. Even though it was a chilly evening, she felt like a boil-in-the-bag meal. Perhaps she was more nervous than she realised.

She waited for the right moment to approach Margaret, leaving it as late in the evening as she could before lightly touching her elbow to signal for her to follow her. A quiet corner of the gazebo beside the bar was the best place for this type of conversation. Her phone was in her hand and recording.

Margaret was eager to follow Katherine as she hoped she would be, and the sway in her movements indicated she'd had more than enough to drink, perhaps too much.

"So, did you have a good Christmas? Got everything

you wanted and more I hope," Margaret slurred, taking a sip from her newly refilled glass of Prosecco.

Katherine wondered if she was referring to her gift.

"I didn't quite get everything I wanted, no, Margaret." Katherine gave her the eyes; a look Rebecca had said no woman could resist.

"Oh," Margaret said, moving closer to Katherine.

Her heart pounded at the betrayal. Knowing how important it was to extract what she could from Margaret, she pushed on.

Katherine prepared her most sensual tone before replying. "I would have liked to have thanked the person who informed the General Medical Council about me and Anna over the summer. It changed my life in a way I would never have expected. It brought me closer to the abbey, and to you, and I will be forever grateful to them." Katherine allowed her hand to stroke Margaret's and the deep breath that Margaret took told her it was having the intended effect.

"Thank them? You wouldn't be… angry?"

Katherine softened her face and widened her lips as authentically as she could. "No, of course not, who could blame them, we were in the wrong after-all. I would just like the chance to show them my appreciation for changing my life for the better."

Margaret giggled and then covered her mouth, leaning a little too close to Katherine for her liking. She reeked of Prosecco; the vapours so strong they were heady.

Katherine resisted the urge to back away.

Margaret thought for a moment before speaking. "I

have a little confession… it was me." Margaret plunged forward and kissed Katherine.

She had meant to push her back if Margaret tried anything like that but was distracted by Anna delivering some more bottles of Prosecco at the bar. By the time she'd realised Margaret was attached to her face and pulled away, Anna had disappeared. She would reluctantly have to wait to talk to her; Margaret was ripe for further confession, and Katherine was getting every minute of it recorded on her phone. It hadn't occurred to her that Margaret would be so forthcoming with the truth, she had planned other lines of questioning and was now a little off guard. Perhaps Margaret had been desperate to get her feelings off her chest.

Katherine stepped back a little and continued her gentle coercion with a light brushing up and down Margaret's arm. "And the ring in my drawer, did you take it? Would you prefer it on your finger?" She took Margaret's hand, hoping to entice her further towards the truth.

"I might have had something to do with it. You must admit; we are better suited than you and Anna. She's a little immature for a woman like you," Margaret replied, swaying a little as she spoke.

Katherine could feel her blood boiling at Margaret's comment. She pushed her back with her finger. "She's ten times the woman you could ever be," Katherine replied through gritted teeth. She'd already noticed a few people look in their direction and she didn't need an audience.

Margaret pulled herself upright at Katherine's change

of tone. Katherine moved closer to her and whispered in her ear.

"You listen up and listen carefully. I've just recorded your little confession. I wonder what the other trustees would say if I played it to them."

Margaret blinked rapidly, trying to catch up to the conversation. "But... I put it back. Kat, I love you, I thought you felt—"

"You thought wrong, and you can take this." Katherine took Margaret's hand and placed the jewellery box firmly into it.

Margaret's face dropped at the realisation that she had been tricked. "You two won't last," she sneered.

"You won't last. Either you quit or become a silent trustee. It's your choice. To be honest I'd be happy to never see you again. You've betrayed my trust and that's unforgivable."

"I think I'd better leave," Margaret said, with more control over herself. There was nothing better to sober someone up than reality crashing them back down to earth.

"Not until after the fireworks. You'll put your game face back on and do what is needed to make this night a success for Anna. It's the least you can do for us, and Margaret, one last thing, only my friends can call me Kat!"

Katherine strode away from Margaret as her mouth dropped open. She only had one thing on her mind: she needed to find Anna and explain what she had seen in the gazebo. She headed back to the visitor centre, assuming Anna would be there. Carrie was directing some stragglers to the far end of the site to watch the firework display.

"Carrie, have you seen Anna?"

"Yes, she was heading up to the top of the site with the fireworks chap. It's nearly midnight. Is everything okay?"

"I hope so. Thank you."

Katherine headed back the way she came, frantically looking for any sign of Anna. She knew Anna had seen Margaret kiss her, and she would have to hope that Anna understood it wasn't her kissing Margaret. If she ever needed Anna to show that trust she said she had in her, it was now. At least she had the recording on her phone to prove what she'd done and why, if needed.

A check of her watch told her it was three minutes until midnight. The fireworks were planned to be set off on the hour. What Anna must be thinking played on her mind as she scoured the crowd. She'd witnessed everything playing out as she had predicted, and more importantly, she had been right all along.

The site filled with the voices of the crowd as they counted down the last ten seconds of the year. Silence then fell momentarily as the first fireworks shot up into the sky. A bang echoed around the site and large shower of light fell, illuminating the abbey to the cheers of the crowd. Katherine took the opportunity to scan the site. She spotted Anna alone in the chapel window where they had once sat just after they met. She pushed her way through the crowds unnoticed, their attention focused on the sky.

CHAPTER 15

*A*nna leaned back against the side of the window ledge and hugged her tucked-up legs. This spot in the chapel had become her favourite place in the abbey, a place she could think and relax. Not only was it one of the furthest points away from the visitor centre, making it the quietest place on the site, four walls remained of the room, giving it some shelter. It always reminded her of the time she and Katherine finally landed on the same wavelength.

She needed a few moments away from the visitors. She was exhausted and hadn't had five minutes to take in the evening's events, let alone sit down.

The evening had been a whirlwind of answering questions about the new barn, chatting to locals she hadn't seen for years and fetching and carrying supplies for the bars. She had particularly enjoyed watching the children play together in the dark, duelling with the glowsticks she had the foresight to bulk buy earlier in the month.

It reminded her of being a child at new year. The

excitement of staying up late and welcoming another year in, then feeling a little adult for being up after midnight. The children were what she missed most about being a tour guide. She loved watching their faces light up as she gave them an exciting snippet of information about the abbey or a scary ghost story.

The fireworks were going down a treat with the sound of oohs and aahs at all the right moments. Her thoughts drifted to Katherine as multicoloured lights glowed in the sky above her. She had been busy with Margaret in the VIP tent the last time she saw her. So much for her hopes for them to enjoy the fireworks together and her plan to propose to Katherine at midnight. It seemed the two of them were destined to misfire.

She scanned the site with each bright firework in the hope of spotting her. A shuffle by the doorway told Anna she didn't need to look any further; she'd been found.

"There you are. I've been looking all over for you," Katherine said between panted breaths.

Anna glanced over at her and then turned away to watch the fireworks.

Katherine joined her, mirroring Anna's position on the opposite side of the large window.

Anna could feel Katherine eyes boring into her, no doubt trying to gauge her reaction. She'd let Katherine speak first; she knew she had a habit of blowing up over situations when it would have been better to listen and allow her to explain.

"You were right. She does have feelings for me, and she reported me — us — to the GMC. I'm sorry I didn't believe you at first; I can't believe how blind I was."

Anna fought against the tightness in her lips as they attempted to smile. She'd been right all along, and more importantly, now Katherine knew it for certain.

Anna waited for a silent moment between the fireworks before speaking. "Sometimes it's good to be blind. It allows us to see the best in people rather than the worst."

A firework shot up into the sky, screaming as it went.

"I want her gone, Katherine," Anna continued, the tone of her voice deeper than before.

"She will be."

Anna gazed back at the fireworks. "How is her reporting you to the GMC going to get her out of our lives? She did the right thing. We can hardly use it against her."

"She took something precious from me. Something I'd planned on giving you in Bath."

Anna's heart pounded. This was the first acknowledgement she'd had of a proposal other than her dad's sleepy mutterings.

Katherine continued. "I tricked her into admitting everything to me in exchange for letting her think it might get her somewhere with me."

"You temptress," Anna replied, finally allowing the smile to release itself.

Katherine laughed; it sounded almost like a release of relief that Anna wasn't flying off the handle. "I'm sorry you had to watch her kiss me. That must have hurt."

Anna shrugged. "I knew you had it all under control." She knew this to be true. She wasn't simply trying to make

Katherine feel like she was trusted; she did trust her. She trusted her to protect their relationship with everything she had. She could feel Katherine's eyes boring into her again.

"Watch the fireworks, not me; this is the end," Anna said, turning to her.

Katherine shook her head. "No, it's the beginning. I love you, Anna, and I want to spend the rest of my life with you."

Anna turned away to catch the final fireworks as a large spray of lights threw themselves into the sky. "I have one condition," she replied quickly before Katherine could continue.

"Anything."

The spray of crackling lights fell slowly across the site, and the audience fell into a moment of silence.

Anna looked back to Katherine and met her gaze. "That you spend it as my wife."

Katherine ejected a small cry. The light from the fireworks reflected in the tears that were forming in her eyes. She wiped them and covered her enormous smile with her hand. Anna took her hand so she could see her face.

"Was that a yes?" Anna asked.

Katherine nodded and then managed to speak. "Yes." She pulled Anna's face towards her and kissed her, holding her to her lips until the crackling of the fireworks died away and were replaced with the sound of the crowd cheering. "That's all for you, that is."

Anna smiled. She had managed to pull it all off and more. She had asked Katherine to marry her, not the other way round. "I'm sorry if I stole your proposal and that you didn't get a chance to ask me in Bath."

Katherine frowned at her. "How did you know?"

"Dad muttered something at the hospital about you asking me something, and I put two and two together. You certainly get ten out of ten for your choice of location." A thought sprang into Anna's mind. "Rewind a second. What did Margaret take?"

"The ring I had planned on proposing with." Katherine's hand dove into her pocket. She placed the two rings on the palm of her hand and pointed to the one with the diamond.

"What's this one?" Anna asked, pointing at the other. "It looks like a replica of Jane Austen's turquoise ring. It's gorgeous."

Katherine twisted her head; the corners of her mouth lifted a little. "It is. I bought it in the shop as a replacement as I thought I'd lost the other one. It turned out she'd taken it so I couldn't use it to propose in Bath. She put it back after, of course."

"Little did she know how determined our Katherine was that she'd buy another. How did she even know you had it or your intentions?" Anna's face dropped. "You didn't tell her your plan, did you?"

"Of course not. I think she must have overheard me on the phone to the jewellers." Katherine paused. "Thinking about it, she could have even snooped in my emails." Katherine shuddered. "Its absence did initially make me wonder if it was a sign, especially after Harry." Katherine took Anna's hand. "Even with all that, I knew how I felt and what I wanted."

Anna scrunched her face up; she felt a little teary. "I haven't bought you a ring at all and you've bought me two."

Katherine smiled. "I don't mind. Which one would you like? I really like the diamond, if you don't, then I won't be offended."

Anna picked the diamond ring up and placed it on Katherine's finger. "If you like this one, you have it. I'm paying you back for it, though. I prefer this one." Anna held the replica ring out to Katherine.

She took it and placed it on Anna's finger. "I think this one suits you better actually." She kissed the back of her hand. "Hang on, when did Harry tell you I was going to propose?"

"On Christmas day."

Katherine's mouth opened. "You've known since then. Have you been planning to steal my proposal since then too?"

Anna shrugged. "Pretty much."

Katherine tapped her on the nose. "Sneaky."

"Come on, we better help clear up. This is still my show, you know."

They walked back hand in hand amongst the ruins, away from the crowds all trying to exit at the same time. As they reached the car park, Anna pulled Katherine to a stop. "I just want a moment to take in all these happy faces in case this is my last event."

Carrie appeared from behind them with an enormous torch. "Margaret's quit. Someone saw her clear her desk. She left before the fireworks even finished. Are you going to be our new boss, Katherine?"

"I'm sure you'll hear everything in due course, Carrie. Happy New Year," Katherine replied, leading Anna away.

Carrie nodded. "And to you both."

Anna wiggled the ring on her finger at Carrie as she walked away.

Carrie's mouth dropped open, and she wiggled on the spot. "Congratulations."

"Thanks," Anna called back to her.

Katherine whispered in her ear. "How can I take Margaret's job when I'm responsible for her losing it?"

"You're not responsible; she is," Anna said stiffly under her breath.

"I suppose you're right, as always apparently, and you made a success of tonight. If… if I'm offered Margaret's role, I'll appoint you into your role."

"Isn't that going to be a conflict of interest?"

Anna felt her hand being squeezed.

"I think you've earned it off your own back, don't you?"

"Yes, I rather think I have," Anna replied, squeezing Katherine's hand in return. She looked around, realising they had passed the visitor centre entirely and proceeded further on to Abbey Barn. "We've missed our stop."

Katherine paused. "No, we haven't. I led you here to make a proposal. Since it was originally my idea and I have yet to make one."

Anna turned to face her. "You know I'll say yes to anything you ask."

"We get married here at the abbey. I can't think of anywhere nicer than the barn for a wedding breakfast. I'd have to check with our rather sexy events manager, but I think we have our pick of dates."

"I'll have to check my diary." Anna leaned forward and placed her lips against Katherine's.

Her birthday felt so long ago, and the summer belonged to another aeon. So much had happened since she met Dr Atkinson, and she could not wait to spend every lovely, long, and even frustrating moment with her.

REVIEWS

If you enjoyed this book please consider leaving me a
review on Amazon, BookBub or Goodreads. Just a rating
or a line is fine. They really make a huge impact for
authors.

AMAZON REVIEW LINK

JOIN MY READERS CLUB

If you'd like to hear about my new releases, sign up to my Readers Club and receive a FREE sapphic romance, *The Third Act…*

At the suggestion of her daughter, Amy, widowed Fiona attends an art course at the local college where she meets the confident, inspirational teacher, Raye.
Raye awakens feelings long suppressed, but as Fiona rediscovers her sexuality, fear grows over how Amy will react. Can Fiona find the courage to follow her heart, or will she be destined to spend her third act alone?

Absolutely loved this book! Great story line, well developed characters and beautifully crafted. It is really refreshing to see the older lesbian represented for a change !

www.emilybanting.co.uk/freebook

NUNSWICK ABBEY SERIES BOOK
THREE

FORGIVE NOT FORGET

Join Anna and Katherine as Nunswick Abbey opens for the spring amidst building work, archaeological excavations, and vandalism.

When an old school friend returns to the village with her family, Anna begins to question her long held vision of her future.

Old wounds are reopened for Katherine when she's presented with an opportunity to face her past head on. Can Anna convince her to take it and finally confront her fears?

With Anna dreaming of the future and Katherine consumed by the past, can they get on the same page and decide what life they want to build together?

PREORDER HERE

www.ingramcontent.com/pod-product-compliance
Lightning Source LLC
Chambersburg PA
CBHW030838200726

48285CB00007B/2476